Omega on the Run

New Alphas: Book 2

逃走中

Kaydee Robins

Omega on the Run

Copyright © 2020 Kaydee Robins Publishing

All rights reserved. No part of this publication may be reproduced, distributed, or transmitted in any form or by any means, including photocopying, recording, or other electronic or mechanical methods, without the prior written permission of the publisher, except in the case of brief quotations embodied in critical reviews and specific other noncommercial uses permitted by copyright law.

All names, characters, and references to the real world are written in a fictitious manner. Any use of trademarks has not been authorized and is used strictly for fictitious purposes and is in no way associated with the owners of said trademarks.

Dedication

Jessi —

You saved my life in more ways than one. Thank you for rescuing me and loving me when I was broken.

— Linc

Author's Note

Omega on the Run is the second installment of *The New Alphas* series. While you can read each book as a standalone HEA, I recommend reading them in the correct order; otherwise, you chance spoilers.

Due to the quick-pace, live births may not be included in each book; however, there is an epic finale in the last segment where you will meet all the little ones as they are born. There is even a bonus baby. And you know we all like bonus babies.

So, without further ado, please turn the page and enjoy Lincoln and Jessi's story.

Contents

Chapter 1 6
Chapter 2 9
Chapter 3 14
Chapter 4 18
Chapter 5 23
Chapter 6 31
Chapter 7 36
Chapter 8 40
Chapter 9 44
Chapter 10 50
Chapter 11 54
Chapter 12 58
Chapter 13 62
Chapter 14 66
Chapter 15 72
Chapter 16 77
Chapter 17 81
Chapter 18 85
Chapter 19 89
Chapter 20 93
Thank You 97
Japanese Terms 98
Sneak Peek 99
Other books by Kaydee Robins 103
About the Author 104

Chapter 1

The room was dark and damp against Linc's skin, as it always was. He shivered against the bare mattress, huddling against himself in his threadbare clothes. He wrapped his arms around his skinny legs, trying to make friction to warm himself up, but it was useless. The wind howled against the only window in his cell of a room. He only had a bare mattress with no sheets in his room, and it was stained from the bodily fluids of himself and his master.

The wind pushed against the single-pane window, causing it to groan in protest. Moonlight his only source of light. He tried to close his eyes and sleep; it was the only reprieve from his daily nightmare. On good days he ate twice a day and allowed to use the bathroom once. The rest of the time, he had to piss in the bucket in his room. On bad days they, deprived of food and water, had to shit in the bucket before Harvey fucked him relentlessly.

He usually at least had a blanket to curl up under at night, but when he didn't behave, his master took it away from him. Since he tried to escape last night, he was now without his blanket for a week.

Linc had no idea how long he had been in this horrid place, but the memories of his family were fading. He barely remembers a time when he was happy but held on to what he could. He pressed his face into his knees and instantly winced from the bruises on his face.

"Fuck," he whispered. Tears trailed down his cheeks. "I'm going to get you out of here. We're going to get out of here," he cried. He had been whispering that to his stomach the last week since he found out he was pregnant with that bastard's baby. He would figure out how to kill himself and the baby before he ever let that man get his hands on his child.

The tree outside his window knocked across the window. He was sure that Harvey and his wife were asleep already. He didn't hear any other sounds in the night. Harvey had replaced the window in his room a long time ago with a sealed window the first time he tried to escape. He used to have the run of the house but lost his privileges as time went on. But still, he wouldn't let Harvey win. He would be defiant until the day he escaped or the day he died.

The storm was fierce tonight; Harvey mentioned that the wind outside was as strong as a tornado. Linc had survived a few tornadoes when he was younger and free. There had been a few more since Harvey had kidnapped him, but this was the strongest so far.

Linc closed his eyes, letting the gentle tap, tap, tap against the window lull him to sleep. He tossed and turned against the mattress, dreaming of his family, of his brother's smile. Yet, like always, the smiles turned to horror when the gunshot ripped through his brother's torso. He woke with a start before the blood could start ruining his brother's shirt.

That was weird. Linc looked around to see what woke him before the screams in his head. The door bolted shut from the other side. He stood up and stretched; he didn't get that much sleep, but it was better than some nights. Linc walked towards the window, something he did after he woke. The boy gazed at the moon and stars, hoping it would replace whatever horrors he would face for the day.

Yet, this time as he approached the window, he cried out and fell to his hands. He clamped his right hand over his mouth, not wanting anyone to hear his cries; it was better that way. His other hand hit something on the ground. He closed his hand around it and gasped when he felt pain and the trickle of blood.

"What the hell?" he muttered to himself. He didn't dare speak any louder.

He stood up, wincing when his foot hit more glass. Linc realized that the window had shattered while he was asleep. A grin spread across his thin lips. If he had his blanket, he would have grabbed it and taken it with him, but didn't, so he scurried out the window. If he was quiet, he could get far away before the morning, hopefully anyway. With the clouds overhead, he couldn't tell where the moon was in the sky.

Linc knew this was the only chance, though he couldn't wait another second. If Harvey discovered the window in the morning and Linc hadn't tried to run, perhaps Linc would get a reward. Maybe it would be lunch for a few days. But Linc wanted freedom;

everything was worth it.

He finally pushed himself with the last of his strength through the window. He rolled onto the roof, laying there for a minute catching his breath.

When he was breathing normally again, he carefully made his way to the front of the house, away from Harvey's room. Jumping from the overhang above the kitchen made it a little higher than if he went to the back of the house. But Harvey would be sure to hear him if he tried that way.

He turned around, dangled his feet over the ledge, and slid down until he was hanging from his fingertips. It was another four feet to the ground. He bent his knees to tuck them up to himself before releasing his hands.

He crumbled in pain, biting his tongue so he wouldn't make a sound. Hopefully, the storm covered up the thump he made. He laid there for a few minutes until he caught his breath, and the pain abated a bit.

The wind beat against the dreadful ramshackle farmhouse as he ran into the darkness of the night. The last thing he remembered before passing out was the rising sun and his feet hitting the pavement.

Chapter 2

The road was long without his husband. It had been a year since Jessi and his late husband, Geoff, had been attacked outside of San Francisco. This trip was only the second trip in his new rig without his husband's company, and he didn't like the silence. Not at all. Yet, he would continue to drive for his rescuers for the rest of his life.

The Yakuza was his family now; Takamori Enoki men had saved him from certain death and nursed him back to health. He owed the small town everything. So, he ran a hand over his bearded face, trying to wake himself. He had been on the road for twelve hours now.

Since DOT (Department of Transportation) no longer existed, he didn't have to follow their guidelines. Even though he should follow them, they had been in place for a reason. People got tired; it was inevitable.

With the interstates being desolate and prone to attacks, he kept to the back roads. But that meant it took him longer to get across the country and deliver the goods in the trailer. Thankfully, it was the beginning of his trip.

He exchanged produce for other items that didn't have an expiry date. Driving from the west coast to the east coast, he delivered much-needed products. In exchange, he received items his town couldn't produce.

He bounced from small towns to larger cities and everything in between. Eventually, his trailer was full of random things needed by the city. He often thought he was on an episode of Barter Kings.

The sound of his tires hitting the rumble strip caused Jessi to jolt awake. He scrubbed down the front of his face again and slowed. The rig jerked as he pulled off the road into the grass.

His headlights hit something lying in the grass about a hundred yards ahead of him. He slammed the breaks to keep from hitting whatever it was. His forty-year-old eyesight was not what it used to be. Since Lens Crafters no longer existed, he couldn't order a pair of glasses.

Once his truck came to a stop, he threw the transmission into park, turned the engine off, and climbed out of the truck. He left the headlights on, so he could see. Once he got closer to the object, he realized that it was a person.

A small, beautifully pale man. He was covered in bruises, but his face was relaxed as he slept. His clothes were threadbare and dirty. He had no shoes on. Clearly, this man needed his help, and Jessi was a sucker for the weak. Although, he had a feeling that this younger man was anything but weak.

The boy was shivering in his sleep. Jessi bent down and mildly shook the man's shoulder, trying to wake him. "Hey," he whispered, staying as far away from the man as he could. Jessi knew what he looked like; he didn't want to startle the young man if he could help it.

Jessi whisked the shabby black hair out of the man's face when he didn't awake. "Come on, sweetheart, wake up for me," he said, caressing the man's cheek. But the man still didn't wake.

He spent several minutes trying to wake the man with no avail. "Well, let's get you into my rig then," he sighed, hoping the man didn't wake up while he was in Jessi's arms. He slid his lumberjack sized arms under the man's tiny body and lifted him gently. The guy couldn't have weighed over one-hundred pounds.

The man's head flopped on his chest. Jessi cradled him in his arms like he was precious cargo, and to Jessi, he already was. This man was Jessi's type and reminded Jessi a lot of his late husband. He whimpered as Jessi made his way back to his truck but didn't wake.

After getting him settled into his truck, Jessi climbed into the other side. Then maneuvered them into the sleeping area. There were two bunks, but the top one wasn't made as he always slept on the bottom and having never had company. His bed was covered in blankets and was very cozy. It had to be since he was on the road for months at a time.

Without thought, Jessi placed the young man in the bottom bunk and then grabbed the first aid kit and a rag. He dug out his camp stove, a small pan and a jug of water. After a few minutes, he had warm water that he dipped the rag in and started cleaning the man's feet. They were dirty, scraped up, and bleeding from whatever journey the man had been.

When he was done cleaning the boy's feet, he placed bandages on the wounds before putting a pair of socks on the man's feet. Jessi wondered what his name was already becoming enraptured with the boy.

Fuck, Jessi, don't think like that, he thought. He's running from something; he will not want you like that. Jessi shook his head as he started working on the wounds on the man's face and arms. He assumed the man was hurt in other places but wasn't about to strip him to find out.

Once all the visible wounds were taken care of, Jessi covered him in the blankets. He pulled the top one off for himself and threw it on the top bunk.

He reached for the drinking water and lifted the man's head and poured a bit of water in his mouth. The young man swallowed but still didn't wake, but he groaned and licked his lips. Once he got water into the man, he laid his head back on the pillow and tucked the covers back around him.

Jessi then went about making his dinner, ramen, before turning in for the night. He left a bottle of drinking water that would be in the man's line of sight. Then locked the front doors before climbing onto the top bunk. He usually stripped to his birthday suit before sleeping. However, he didn't have sheets or a pillow, and he only had one blanket, so he left his clothes on and used his jacket as a pillow.

He tossed and turned for about an hour before falling into a restless sleep. His mind kept drifting back to the night he lost his husband.

逃走中

The road was dark; Geoff sat beside him in the passenger seat, smiling at him. He had made a joke about how the city looked so different from how it was when they were kids. Before the pandemic destroyed everything, they knew.

Jessi's restaurant, Iced Island, which was on Long Island, had only been opened for three years. Then the pandemic broke out. It only took two months for his sales to drop to the point he had to close the restaurant.

Two months after marrying his husband, they invested all their savings into a big rig. They made it their mission to deliver supplies to people in need.

Almost twenty years passed as the two of them zigzagged across the United States. They watched as cities slowly fell apart as people died. Jessi and Geoff were one of the lucky ones. They knew the risks of continuing their work, but they did it anyway. It would be safer for them to go underground, as many Americans had done, but they persevered. So, to lose his lover like he haunted him still a year later.

Jessi pulled to a stop as the pickup trucks surrounded their rig. San Francisco was dangerous. They knew that the Irish mob was running it and that they were ruthless. But he thought the Irish would leave the supply drivers alone, as they had in the past.

However, the minute they pulled within the city limit, trucks started following them. Then, blocking the side streets, he had no choice to go to one location where another mob of trucks waited. Outside the trucks were several angry, redheaded alphas and old-worlders. Jessi knew they made a mistake. They should have never taken the job to deliver supplies inside the city.

As soon as they stopped the rig, the driver's door was ripped open, followed seconds later by the passenger door. They pulled his tiny husband from his seat before he toppled out the door.

He saw under the rig as people kicked, punched, and raped his husband while taking his own beating. He fought with everything he had, but there were too many of them. His head pounded from the damage to his face, but all he cared about was getting to his husband. As quickly as it started, it was over.

Acid air filled his lungs when he could finally stand. He broke his right leg. A few teeth were missing, and he could barely breathe, but he hobbled over to the passenger side. He steadied himself against the hood of the truck when he saw his lover's battered body. He dropped to his knees and cradled Geoff's head in his lap. "Baby, I'm here. Hang on."

Jessi looked up to take in his surroundings. The last thing he saw before blacking out was the flames blazing feet above the hood of his rig. No wonder it smells, he thought.

Jessi woke up, screaming Geoff's name. His throat was hoarse and dry. He looked around him and realized he was back in the present, and Geoff was long gone.

It took a few minutes for him to calm. His heart racing at the genuine feeling that everything had just happened again. It had been months since he dreamed about that night, and he was unsure what brought it on.

Once his heart rate returned to normal, he climbed out of the bunk and checked on the kid. He was still sound asleep. Jessi brushed the hair from his face again and stared at the unblemished portions of the man's face. His creamy ivory skin was beautiful. Jessi wanted nothing more than to wrap his powerful arms around this boy and take care of him. To make sure nothing else ever happened to him.

He tried to wake him again, to no avail. The man must be exhausted. Or he has a head injury, the voice in his head added. "Fuck!" He scrubbed his hand over his face, debating on what to do. He should find a doctor and make sure the man was okay. But he wasn't sure whom he could trust around here.

If he turned around and went straight home, it would still take a day to get there. He would be going back with a mostly empty trailer, a waste of gas.

Whenever he dreamed about the night his husband died, he could not sleep afterward. Therefore, he let out a sigh before putting on his percolator to make coffee. He then pulled out the eggs and bacon to make a quick breakfast. He made enough for the man for when he woke and sat it aside.

Dawn was on the horizon as he finished his breakfast. He poured the plain black coffee into his thermos and then took the dirty dishes outside to wash. He was in the middle of northern Utah, in a valley surrounded by mountains. The mountains were beautiful, with the tips covered in snow. The cool morning breeze gave him a chill as he finished the dishes.

He climbed back into the rig and stored all his dishes and the camp stove. He forced a cup of water down the man's throat. Then secured his plate of food for the ride before he climbed back into the driver's seat.

His best choice was to continue on his way doing the deliveries. He could take care of the man in the back himself once he woke. He could also ask people for doctors. The man was running from someone, and he didn't want to tip that someone off. He turned his music down real low as he started his day on the road.

Chapter 3

It was warm, really warm. Linc hadn't remembered being this warm since before Harvey had taken him. He groaned as he rolled over in pain, but it was so warm he didn't care. Then it registered; there was a vibration like he was in a car.

He panicked before sitting up. Hitting his head on something above him. He let out a yelp before promptly clamping his hand over his mouth.

"Whoa," a deep rich voice called over the loud noise filling whatever room Linc was in. But that made little sense. He could feel the vibrations of a car below me, how was he in a room too.

Against his better judgment, Linc opened his eyes. It surprised him to see a blanket over him. He looked around and found that he was in a small room. The bed he was on was soft but stiff, and it was small. The room was only as wide as the bed, and there were only a few feet in the open space.

Suddenly, the vibrations under him stop, and he heard a whooshing sound. The light in the room dimmed as something filled the only entryway to the tiny room. Linc looked up to see a giant frame standing in the way. A lumberjack of a man, to be exact. Linc couldn't see many of his features in the light except for the dark hair and face full beard.

Linc reacted without thought and curled in a ball as tight as he could.

"Whoa, it's okay," the giant said. He held his hands up, showing he had nothing in his hands. Linc didn't trust him though and stayed huddled on the bed, clutching the blanket.

The man squatted down in front of Linc. The extra light allowed him to see more of his face. He hid most of it beneath his unruly black beard that was a few inches long. His hair was black with silver flecks throughout, showing his age.

He had a kind smile, but that didn't mean much to Linc since Harvey seemed nice until he wasn't. Linc could feel his hands shaking in the blanket. He wasn't sure what this man wanted, but he was afraid to ask too. But he didn't half to.

After half a minute, the man spoke again, "my name is Jessi." He whispered as if he was talking to a scared kitten, which was mostly correct in Linc's case. "Would you like some water?"

Linc would have loved some water, but he didn't want to owe this man anything. If the man gave him water, what would he want in return? The man, Jessi, Linc thought in his head, opened the bottle when there was no response and took a swig.

"See, perfectly fine," Jessi said, pulling the bottle from his lips. He didn't ask Linc again if he wanted the water. He held it out in front of Linc so he could grab it quickly.

Linc snatched the bottle before the man took it away. He took a drink. It was cold and felt excellent against his dry throat. He started drinking more.

"Hang on, slow down," Jessi said. "You don't want to make yourself sick."

Linc slowed down and took small sips for a few minutes. Silence hung between the two men. "Linc," Linc whispered.

"Linc," Jessi mimicked. "Is that short for Lincoln?"

He nodded.

"Well, Linc, are you hungry?"

He nodded again.

Jessi reached over to a cabinet and grabbed a plate. He sat it on the bed. He filled the dish with bacon and eggs. "It's a little cool. I made it a few hours ago."

Linc didn't care. It was the most food he'd seen on a plate in a while. He picked up the fork and ate the perfectly seasoned eggs. After they settled, he consumed two pieces of bacon as well, then drank more water.

"I'm guessing you probably need to use the bathroom; you must go outside or pee in a bottle. Your feet were banged up bad, so I don't know if you're up for walking outside. I can help you if you like."

The pain hit Linc as soon as Jessi mentioned his feet. He had been so used to being scrapped up and beaten that he ignored the discomfort, mostly. But having this caring man talk about it made it come to the forefront of his mind.

Linc released the blanket and moved his feet off the bed. He noticed he had socks on, and his toes were warm. Again, something that he wasn't used to anymore. He tried to stand up and collapsed. Yet, instead of crashing to the floor, Jessi swept him up in strong arms.

"Whoa, there, sweetheart. Careful," he sat Linc back down on the bed. "Here." He handed Linc an empty bottle and turned.

Considering Linc had pissed in a bucket for years, this was easy. He took care of business and then sealed the bottle.

"Thanks," he squeaked.

The brute of a man turned around again. "I dressed the injuries I could see, but I, um, didn't want to remove your clothes." Jessi's cheeks were pink, and he was running his hand along the back of his neck. "I don't have any pants that will fit you, but this should cover everything. There's a truck stop that's still opened in about three-hundred miles. We can stop there and get you clothes and shoes. But for now, you can wear my shirts. And um, I'd like to check out your injuries if you'll let me."

Linc didn't know what to do with the information. Jessi was just staring at him like he was waiting for an answer. But Linc wasn't about to get naked in front of a strange man, no matter how nice he seemed. "This is it," Linc said, pointing to cuts and bruises on his arms and face. There were several cuts across his back that were still opened from when Harvey whipped him last. But he did not want this kind man knowing about them.

Jessi looked like he didn't believe Linc's answer, but after a second, he nodded. "Alright, then. I'll let you get dressed. Here's a washcloth," he said, handing Jessi a dingy water washcloth. It was damp.

The giant man grabbed the piss bottle and turned. Linc heard a door open and then shut, then he was by himself. He pulled his shirt over his head and winced at the pain lancing through him. He took the washcloth and wiped down his back as best as he could. Linc cringed when the cloth went over one of the opened wounds.

He slipped Jessi's shirt on and then stood using his toes only, so he didn't put any pressure on the wounds on his feet. The shirt fell to his knees. He reached under it and yanked off the dirty pants before sitting back down.

Linc cleaned up as best as he could around his dick and balls. The door opened. "You all done in there?" Jessi called.

"Yes."

Linc could finally figure out he was in the back of a big rig. He saw a few in town when he was little, but never up close. A minute later, Jessi was back in the entry way to the sleeping cabin. There was a glint in Jessi's eyes that were soft, but Linc didn't know what it meant.

"You want to ride upfront with me?"

Linc nodded. He went to stand again, but before he could, Jessi swept him up and spun. Linc had no choice but to wrap his arms around Jessi's neck. Jessi walked the few feet to the front and deposited him in the passenger chair.

He grabbed an extra water bottle and handed it to Linc before sitting down in the driver's seat. Yet, he didn't start the truck. After a few minutes of silence, he turned to Linc. "So, before I get back on the road, do you want to go with me?"

Linc gulped. He had been asking himself that question since he woke. But if he didn't go with the big man, where would he go, and the man seemed to care. Anything would be better than Harvey finding him. "I'd like to go," he whispered, looking down into his lap.

Jessi wasn't having any of it though he reached over and lifted Linc's face, so they were looking at each other. "Hey, I will not force you ever to do anything you don't want to do, okay?"

Linc nodded and tried to look away.

"I mean it, Linc. If you want to get out, I won't stop you. I won't like it, but I wouldn't stop you."

Something in Jessi's voice sounded sincere, and it made Linc relax. He nodded and then melted into the seat. "Take me away from here as quickly as possible." Linc could still see the same mountain ranges that he'd seen all his life. That meant that Harvey was still close enough to find them if he wanted. But the mountains also looked nearer than they had been.

"Okay," Jessi said, starting the rig. He pulled out onto the road and switched on the music.

Chapter 4

Linc quickly fell asleep once they were back on the road again. Jessi was already becoming fond of the man. His pale skin, point jaw and high cheekbones were all easy on the eyes. However, when Linc opened his eyes, and Jessi saw them for the first time, he was in awe.

At first, Jessi thought his eyes were brown. But what was extraordinary were the specks of green that sparkled when the light hit just right. He imagined that Linc's eyes were hazel. The man couldn't wait to see what they looked like in the sunlight and around other colors.

He drove for hours; Linc must have been exhausted because he didn't stir for a while. Shortly after noon, he heard a coughing sound coming from Linc before Linc sat up suddenly, "pull over."

His face was ashen, and he had a sheen of sweat across his brow as suddenly as he woke. Jessi immediately slowed and pulled over. As soon as Jessi stopped, Linc threw the door opened and climbed out. Jessi was right behind him.

When Jessi reached the other side of the rig, he found Linc retching up his breakfast. He hurried over and pulled back Linc's dirty hair. Jessi needed to find a place that both of them could clean. It had been a while since he had a shower. He usually just cleaned himself with the hand wipes he kept in the rig.

He rubbed Linc's back with his free hand until Linc collapsed onto the ground with a whimper. "Oh, sweetheart," he said, squatting down in front of Linc. The boy looked better now that he had let everything out. "Are you okay?"

Linc nodded. "Sorry," he mumbled.

"Hey, no reason to be sorry," Jessi said. He wasn't usually this gentle with people, but he had a feeling Linc needed it. If he let himself, he could fall for a young man, and that was something he wasn't prepared to do. "Do you want help getting back in the truck?"

"Yes, please, my feet still hurt, but I didn't want to make a mess of your truck."

Jessi picked him up bridal-style gingerly. "Let's get you settled; then I think I have ginger ale in the cab somewhere."

"What's that?"

"It will help with your nausea. There's a small lake up ahead; we'll go there and clean up, okay. Here, wrap your arms around my neck," Jessi said as he adjusted Linc, so he was facing him. Linc followed his direction and wrapped his arms around his neck. Then his legs around his midsection.

Jessi held onto Linc with one hand and reached up to the handle with the other. He stepped up on the first Nerf bar, hoisting them up like Linc weighed nothing. He climbed onto the second Nerf bar and sat Linc down. Linc looked up at him with such trust. He leaned down without thinking and kissed the boy's forehead.

"Thank you," the boy whispered.

"You're welcome."

He jumped down from the highest Nerf bar as he often did and walked around to the driver's side. Bypassing his seat, he rummaged in the back a few minutes until he found it a bottle of ginger ale. He only had the one, but it would help until he could get more. Hopefully, whatever had caused Linc to throw up would be long gone by the time it ran out.

He also found a half pack of saltines. He grabbed another water and returned to the driver's seat. Linc watched him cautiously.

"Here, saltines and ginger ale. They'll help with your tummy." Linc took them quietly, taking a sip of the drink before setting it in the cupholder. Jessi sat the extra water in another cup holder before starting the engine. As a habit, he checked his mirrors for other cars. Even though there weren't many, he still ran across some on his travels.

Linc munch quietly on the saltines for the few minutes it took him to get to the lake up ahead. It was more like a pond, but it was crystal clear. A person could see it from the road if they knew where to look, but it was barely visible. He and Geoff had found it by accident on one of their many trips across the country.

He pulled off the road and parked. "I must carry you, but it's worth it. I promise."

Linc looked apprehensive, but he nodded. Jessi climbed into the back, grabbed a few towels and clean clothes. He stuffed them into a backpack and then threw a bar of soap on top. He didn't have any shampoo, but he learned a long time ago the soap would work in a pinch.

Afterward, Jessi again climbed out of the rig and went around to the passenger side. He opened the door to see that Linc had already spun his legs towards the door.

"Here, put this on, then slip onto my back." Linc took the backpack, slipped it on and then slid out of the truck, wrapping his arms around Jessi's neck. Jessi tucked his arms under Linc's legs. "Ready?"

"Yeah," Linc said.

Jessi locked the door and shut it, tucked his keys into his pocket. Then hiked down the forgotten path to the little lake. He heard Linc inhale deeply behind him.

"It's beautiful out here," Linc said.

And it was. They were just at the foot of the Rockies. The next leg of their journey would take them over the second set of mountains before they left Utah. So, they were surrounded by mountains on either side, far from the desolate area that Jessi had found Linc in.

"I have seen nothing like this," Linc stated in awe.

"No?"

"No, I grew up where you found me. It was okay until—" he paused. Jessi continued down the path, waiting to see if the other man would continue. "Sorry, I don't want to talk about it."

"It's okay, Linc, you don't have to tell me anything you don't want too."

Linc nodded against Jessi's shoulder. Jessi reached the lake. It was stunning; the water was almost crystal clear and surrounded by tall grass. Jessi lowered to a squat, "you must stand on your toes for a minute. I didn't think about that when I had you climb on."

"It's okay." Linc slid off Jessi's back onto his tiptoes and then sat down in the grass. He dropped the backpack off his shoulders, and Jessi turned.

"Do you need help with your clothes?" Jessi asked, not wasting any time by pulling his shirt over his head as he spoke. Since Linc was only wearing one of Jessi's oversized shirts, he ripped it over his head. The magnificent specimen in front of him had already seen the bruising earlier. So, he didn't mind taking his shirt off.

Jessi kicked his shoes off and then slipped his pants down, pulling his boxers with him. His colossal dick hung softly against his left leg. But that's not what caught Linc's attention, Jessi realized. Linc was staring at his leg.

"What happened?" Linc asked.

Jessi looked down at his bare legs. His prosthetic started right below the knee on the left leg. "I was in a car accident a long time ago. My leg was trapped for too long. By the time they used the jaws of life to get me out, it was too late."

"I'm sorry; it's just I've never seen one before," Linc stated. He wasn't being mean about it; it was more of interest than anything.

"Not many younger people have. I imagine that one day this thing will stop working, and I won't be able to get a new one. But let's get you in the water."

Jessi walked over and scooped the now naked Linc up. His skin heated from the contact. If they had met under different circumstances, Jessi wouldn't hesitate to show him what he'd been missing. His cock grew against his will.

"So, can you go into the water with it?"

"No, I'll set you in then take it off before coming in."

Jessi squatted slowly, placing Linc in the soft sand on the water's edge, then sat down just outside the water. He let out a sigh of relief as he took his leg off. It had been on too long. Last night he hadn't wanted to take it off in case Linc needed something.

"It hurts?" Linc asked curiously.

"Yeah, the longer I wear it."

"I don't remember you taking it off last night."

"I didn't; I wanted to help you if needed."

Linc's eyes softened. He looked in awe at the gentle giant that he was coming to see in Jessi. "Don't do that. Can you drive without it on?"

"If I had an automatic rig yeah, but because I don't, I have to wear it," he said as he scooted into the water. He could have stood, but he figured this was easier. "Can you swim?"

Linc blushed, "uh, no."

"That's alright; we'll stay where you can reach," Jessi said. He grabbed soap out of his bag and moved further into the water. Linc followed behind closely. The bottom of his feet didn't hurt as much when he walked through the sand.

When Jessi was up to his waist, he stopped. He waited for Linc to reach him. "Better?"

"Yes, it feels so good. I haven't had a bath in God knows how long. *He* only let me take showers and only once a week if that."

Jessi wanted to ask more about this *he* person. Yet, he didn't want to scare Linc, so he just took Linc's hand in his, "well now you can have them as often as you like."

Linc cheeks heated again. He pulled his hand out of Jessi's and dropped into the water. He may not know how to swim, but Jessi still thought he looked beautiful in the clear water. Jessi cock betrayed him, so he quickly handed Linc the soap and turned.

He dove forward in the water and swam out a few stokes before turning around. He didn't want to get too far away from the boy. When he returned, Linc was staring at him in wonder.

"Can you teach me how to swim?" Linc asked.

"Sure, kid," Jessi replied. He thought the kid moniker would help with his attraction to the boy, but it didn't.

After they finished washing off, Jessi started showing Linc the basics of swimming. Both of them relaxed and enjoying the perfect weather. Jessi hadn't had this much fun since Geoff died. The thought sobered him a bit.

He forced a smile when Linc splashed him. However, he quickly realized that he could smile easily.

Linc suddenly blanched and ran towards the side of the lake. When he got there, he started heaving again without a thought. Jessi followed him, and he held the boy's hair back yet again. Linc wiped his mouth off on the back of his hand when he was done.

"Are you okay?" Jessi asked, pulling Linc into his arms.

The boy went slack against the larger man laying his head on his chest. "Yes, thank you. Stupid morning sickness."

Jessi's arm was wrapped tightly around the boy. It was still weird to him that men could have babies, but he kept his hold on the boy. "You're pregnant?"

Linc started shaking. "Please," he begged.

Jessi held him tighter in response. "Ssh, it's alright. I got you, let it out."

So Linc did. He sobbed against Jessi's chest. When Jessi could no longer hold them both upon his one leg, he pulled Linc down to the ground and sat in the soft sand.

"Please don't make me go back."

"Oh, honey, I would never," he didn't mean to use the term of endearment. It just slipped out. It felt natural to him.

Chapter 5

Linc felt better after his bath in the lake. His cock had stirred a handful of times with Jessi's touch. He didn't want it too, but Jessi was so lovely. He wanted to feel safe in Jessi's arms, but he was scared. Harvey and his wife had been friendly when he first met them too.

Jessi had fixed them lunch once they were back in the rig, and they had eaten quietly. Afterward, Jessi drove them down the road for a few more hours before he parked. Linc climbed into the top bunk at night against Jessi's wishes. However, he hadn't wanted to make Jessi wear his leg at night again.

The man had grumbled the entire time he worked to remove his leg. Even Linc could hear his relief when the thing was off. Linc laid on the bed, staring up at the ceiling for a long while before drifting off to sleep. He felt safe for the first time in a long time.

The next morning Jessi drove a few more hours before they stopped in a small town. They had driven through a handful of cities, including Salt Lake City. They didn't stop in any of them, though, as they were abandoned. This town, though was not, people lined the streets to watch Jessi pull in.

Jessi pulled up to an old grocery store and backed up to the loading dock. "Did you want to stay here? I can pick you up some clothes and shoes, or you can come with me?"

"I'll go," Linc said. He had a pair of Jessi old socks on so his feet wouldn't get dirty. Even though he still had wounds on his feet from the broken glass, he could walk mostly without issue.

He opened the door and climbed down from the rig to be met by Jessi. Another man stood behind Jessi.

"Jessi," an older man said, clapping Jessi on the back. The man was shorter than Jessi and had less hair. He smiled like Linc imagined his grandfather would smile.

"Earl," Jessi replied, pulling the man into a hug. "Nice to see you."

"You too, who's this?"

"This is Linc; he's traveling with me."

Earl gave Linc a once over and smiled sadly. "You think that's safe?"

Jessi looked offended and growled, "I protect what's mine, Earl."

Linc's face turned to that of horror. He pulled out of Jessi's grasp and ran.

"Fuck," Jessi muttered. "Linc! Stop, please." His voice cracked like he was in pain from Linc running away from him.

Linc turned around, frustrated. Jessi was on his heels, proving that Linc probably couldn't outrun him even if he wanted. "You're just like him, why should I stop?" he yelled at the big man.

"Oh, honey." He reached out for Linc's hands and squeezed them gently, "I'm sorry, sweetheart." He brushed the locks of Linc's hair from his face. "I'll never hurt you, Linc, Ever. I just meant that you were mine to protect, yeah?"

Linc didn't respond. He just stared at Jessi's chest and wheezed. Jessi squeezed his hand again, "Lincoln?"

Linc felt his chin being lifted. Jessi's gaze seared his soul. The blackness of his eyes should have felt ominous, but it felt soothing instead. "I promise you I will never hurt you, and you are free to go anytime you want."

Linc said nothing, but he nodded.

The man seemed to realize that Linc was no longer acting like a scared kitten. "Let's get your truck unloaded, yeah?" he said.

"I'm afraid there's not much. I have several crates of veggies. The other towns didn't have much," Jessi said before started walking towards the back of the trailer.

"That's okay, Jessi. You'll stop on your way back, too, right?" Earl replied with a kind smile.

"Of course. Earl, would you take Linc to get clothes and shoes?"

"No," Linc said, causing both men to turn and look at him. "I mean—" he started. He looked nervous now and was holding his hands together so tightly it had to have hurt.

When he didn't continue, Jessi stepped over to him and pulled his hands apart. Linc didn't blink as he watched Jessi's movements. "Kitten, what's the matter?" Jessi asked.

Linc glanced over at the other man before turning back to Jessi then whispered, "don't make me go with him, please?"

Jessi's face turned soft. He reached up and brushed the stray strand out of Linc's face, "oh, kitten, of course. Why don't you go rest in the truck, and I'll come to get you when I'm done unloading?"

Linc didn't know when Jessi had come up with this new pet name, but something lit up inside of him every time Jessi said it. It made him feel welcome and not a burden. "I can help."

"Rest, you're still healing. We'll stay here tonight tomorrow; we drive for four hours before we hit our next stop. You can help then, okay?"

Linc nodded. He knew Jessi was right, so he climbed back into the cab. Jessi had some novels, so he pulled out an old copy of *Gone with the Wind* and started reading it.

逃走中

Linc pulled the blanket over him as he tossed and turned again. It took Jessi an hour to unload the truck with the help of Earl and two other people. They also loaded things back in the rig for Jessie to take. Apparently, Jessi got paid in goods and cash to transport stuff from one place to another.

Jessi told Linc that he filled up the trailer with fresh veggies and other items from the Yakuza. They lived right outside of San Francisco in the country. Linc didn't know what either of those meant, but he didn't ask.

His new friend told him he would spend a few months transporting goods from the west to the east coast. Linc had never seen the ocean before, and he didn't know how big that states were but if it took them months. Wow. Jessi explained that he did a lot of zigzagging and back and forth across the states.

As long as they didn't go anywhere near Harvey's place, he would be okay.

When Jessi said they would stay in town for the night, Linc thought they would sleep in the bunks again. Instead, they had dinner at a nice little Italian restaurant that could still run, albeit with a smaller menu that changed based on ingredients available.

Jessi had taken him to a thrift shop that had secondhand clothes and shoes. They could find Linc a few changes of clothes, a jacket and a pair of tennis shoes. Jessi grabbed him pants that were a bit big. He said that Linc would need him the further he got along in his pregnancy. Linc didn't know because he'd never seen a pregnant person before.

After dinner, they went on a short walk before going to a little motel. The old sign said Motel 8 in front. Earl explained that they hardly ever used it, but they cleaned up a room the minute Jessi rolled into town.

The motel had electricity. Harvey had electricity too, but it had been shoddy. It wasn't like Linc could take advantage of the perks that electricity provided in Harvey's care, anyway. Before they killed his parents, he hadn't lived with electricity. So, this was a luxury to be able to turn the light on with a switch and have an air conditioner.

The rig had AC, but he'd only been with Jessi for a day. So, he wasn't used to it yet.

Jessi introduced him to a TV and a movie. They watched a movie that Jessi loved called *Men in Black*. Linc laughed through most of it. When it was over, they washed up and climbed into bed.

Now though, Linc squirmed as the cool air wafted on him. He reached for the blanket to pull it over him. When he rolled over, he was startled awake by a hand clamping down on his mouth.

His eyes flew open; it was dark, so he couldn't see who had him. The person held him down as he tried to squirm away. He felt cold steel touch his throat.

"Make any noise, and I cut your throat," a scratchy voice hissed quietly.

Linc went slack. He knew he was no match for the man who pulled him to his feet. He could feel the guy's muscles bulging against him. Linc's eyesight was adjusting to the darkness; he could make out the room they were in.

Jessi was still asleep on the other bed if only he could make enough noise that Jessi woke.

"Don't even think about it, Harvey will be pissed if I kill you, but I will if I have too."

Fuck, Fuckity, Fuck. Please, Jessi, please wake up, Linc prayed. The man started pulling him out of the room. He tried to delay the inevitable by fighting, but he was no match for the man holding onto him.

As he got closer to the door, though, he fought harder to get free. He would kill himself before he let Harvey dig his clutches back in. He felt something run down his neck at the same time the hand covering his mouth slipped free. Wasting no time, he screamed,

"Jessi!"

The man cursed and instantly threw him over his shoulder, no longer caring if Linc screamed. Linc was upside down for a few minutes before he literally was torn from the man's back and into Jessi's arms.

Jessi sat him down and immediately pushed Linc behind his bulk. It happened so quickly that Linc was still gasping in a lung full of air when the man tackled Jessi. Both Jessi and the man went to the ground.

"Linc run!" Jessi screamed. Jessi traded blows with the other man as I watched in horror. Jessi was able to roll over and get on top of the man. "Run, Linc, find Earl."

Linc's brain finally kicked in, and he turned to run. He got a few feet before another man grabbed him around the waist. "Jessi!" he screamed. He punched and kicked, but it did no good. This man was just as strong as the other man, if not stronger.

The man pulled him against his chest as he struggled. "Let me go," he yelled, beating uselessly against the man's arm that was holding him.

"What's all this ruckus," someone yelled.

"Go back inside, old man," the man holding Linc replied. "It's none of your business."

"Help me," Linc begged.

"Let him go, Lucan," the old man said.

"Like I told Earl, it's none of your business." The man was still trying to pull Linc towards a car while he ignored Earl.

"Earl, please," Linc begged.

"I said let him go," Earl said steadily. Linc heard something cock behind him.

"This boy belongs to Harvey, Earl. You know what will happen if I let go of him."

"Lucan, you best put that boy down before I take care of you myself. I let you and Harvey run all over this town too long. None of Harvey's crops are worth this boy's life."

The man named Lucan didn't stop, though, "so my son's life is worth less than someone you don't even know?"

"That's your fault, Lucan. You're the one who got into debt with Harvey, not me. I will not let you put this young man in the hands of that evil man; this is your last warning."

Lucan just laughed like he didn't believe the older man. Linc thought that maybe Lucan was right until the gunshot rang out into the night.

Linc toppled to the ground as the man collapsed. He looked over where he last saw Jessi and didn't see him. He scrambled to his feet and ran as fast as possible towards the other man's location. Falling to his knees, he pulled Jessi's head into his lap. The man next to him was beaten to a bloody pulp.

"Jessi, are you okay?"

"Yeah," Jessi replied, sitting. Jessi had a few bruises on his face, and his knuckles looked like hell. Other than that, he looked fine if not, maybe a little disheveled. "Are you okay, kitten? You're the one that was almost kidnapped."

"You and Earl saved me, thank you." Linc placed a kiss on Jessi's cheek.

"You welcome, kitten." Jessi moved his legs to stand up only to realize that his prosthetic was no longer on. "Fuck, my leg."

Linc looked around and found the leg on the other side of the dead man. He handed it to Jessi, who started inspecting it.

"How'd your leg come off?"

"I didn't have time to put the sock on, so it wasn't suctioned properly, it'll be alright. Can you get my sock from the hotel room?"

"Of course," Linc stood up and scurried towards the hotel room. He didn't want to be alone at this moment, but he knew that Jessi couldn't come with him easily without the sock. He was just grateful that Jessi could get his leg on quickly enough to help him.

Once he retrieved the sock, he returned to Jessi. Jessi was murmuring with Earl, "... don't let him out of the rig until your past Denver. Harvey has contacts all over the area."

"Fuck, Earl. I can't lock him up inside the rig that would put him right back where he was with Harvey," Jessi replied.

"No, Harvey's a mean bastard. I had no idea he was keeping a prisoner in his house. Otherwise, I would have rescued Linc a long time ago."

Linc handed Jessi the sock, "you know him?" Linc gulped. He shook. What if Earl just got rid of the others so he could get in Harvey's good graces?

"Breathe, son. Breathe," he heard Earl say. I realized that he was having trouble breathing. He was sucking in air like he couldn't get any in his lungs. "In, and out. Slowly," Earl repeated several times.

Finally, when he could breathe again, he looked up at the older man. "What happened?" he asked shakily.

"You had a panic attack, son." Earl had his hands on Linc's shoulders. "You're safe right now. But Jessi," he said, turning towards the now standing man. "You need to leave now. Remember what I said. I'll take care of Harvey before you get back."

Jessi nodded. "Come on, Linc, let's go." Linc knew he was missing something from the conversation with Jessi and Earl, but he didn't care. He felt safe next to Jessi, but he would feel safer once they were in Jessi's truck alone and on the road.

Jessi headed towards their room, grabbed the things they had taken out of the truck. Then he headed towards the grocery store where he left his vehicle parked. He didn't let go of Linc's hand, not one time. The younger man appreciated the comfort Jessi's warmth gave him.

Jessi helped him up into the truck, not that he needed it, then walked around to the driver's side and climbed in himself. The trailer was now full of handcrafted wooden furniture that Earl's town traded. Some would end up back with the Yakuza, but they would exchange some for other things.

Jessi wasted no time heading out of town. Once they were on the road, Linc asked the question that was burning in the back of his mind. "What was Earl talking about?"

Jessi sighed, "please don't be mad at me."

"Why would I be mad at you?" Linc asked.

"The veggies we just dropped off—" he paused. "They came from Harvey. I had just left his farm when I found you."

Linc sat up, shocked by the information. "What?!"

Suddenly they were stopped, and Jessi placed both hands on his arms, holding him down softly.

"Kitten, listen to me please," Jessi begged.

The pleading in his voice had Linc settling.

"I swear, I had no idea that Harvey was hiding you on his property. I knew he was a cruel man. But I swear to you I didn't know."

Linc nodded. He believed Jessi; he didn't know why he trusted the man, but Jessi had done nothing but to help him.

Jessi settled back into the drivers and took back off, "we need to be careful until after we leave Denver, okay? Harvey has contacts everywhere. We're going to stay out of sight and drop the stuff off and go. I'm sure that Harvey has people like Lucan in every city in Utah. But I can't punish the people that aren't associated with Harvey by not delivering their goods."

"I know Jessi," Linc reached over and squeezed the other man's hand.

Chapter 6

It took them two weeks to reach Colorado Springs. Even with Jessi taking off as soon as the goods were delivered, and new ones were loaded in each town along the way. Usually, it took him three weeks from when he left the small city that Earl lived in. He had no updates from Earl but didn't expect any.

After they made it past Denver, they should be safe to slow back down a little. Except for a few times, Linc stayed in the truck. The times he got out was to bathe with Jessi in lakes when they found them.

His route would bring them back through Earl's town in a few months. But he would call Earl to find out the status of Harvey and his men before he crossed over Denver again. If Harvey hadn't been neutralized by then, he would turn north and go through Montana to return home. He was sure he could find places to trade with up there if he needed too.

Every time he went out, Iggy, his boss, would send him with a list of things they needed in the city. Sometimes he wouldn't find them. Others would require him to veer off his route to find them based on word of mouth. However, he always tried his best to bring back what his town needed.

So far, they had stayed ahead of Harvey and his plans. By now, word had to have reached Harvey that Linc was with Jessi. Harvey might not know the specifics towns Jessi traveled too. But he knew he stopped in Colorado Springs and Denver.

Hopefully, Earl could take care of Harvey before they got into town. However, Jessi wasn't holding his breath.

Jessi reached over and shook Linc awake, "kitten, you need to get in the back. We're coming up on Colorado Springs."

"'Kay," he mumbled. He climbed half asleep from the passenger bucket seat and into the back. "You want breakfast?"

Linc made their breakfast almost every morning after he woke. They had gotten into a routine. Jessi would park for the night; they would eat dinner and hang out. Often Jessi would read a few chapters of a book aloud to Linc before Linc fell asleep against his chest.

At first, they slept separately, but the night after they fled, Linc clung to Jessi desperately. Jessi didn't mind. Against his better judgment, he was already falling for the younger man. Jessi held him tight when Linc whimpered and moaned in his sleep; it seemed to settle the man. Jessi would do anything for Linc.

They would wake about six in the morning. Jessi would drive for two hours before they stopped for breakfast. Linc would fall back asleep in the passenger seat until the sun woke him.

They usually had eggs with a biscuit or toast since most towns had chickens, so they always had a fresh bunch. Sometimes they would have some meat.

If they didn't have any eggs, they would have peanut butter pancakes. They rarely tasted as good as Jessi could make them since they hardly had milk and ended up using water. But it was still better than oatmeal or porridge.

"Always," Jessi said. Linc had mastered cooking while Jessi drove. Jessi could smell the eggs and onions they had picked up yesterday. He could also smell the bacon. That was a rare treat since only a few places along his route had pig farms.

Jessi pulled over a few minutes outside of Colorado Springs and climbed in the back. Linc handed him a plate with scrambled eggs, bacon and a warm biscuit almost as soon as he sat.

"How long are we going to be here?" Linc asked between bites.

"A couple of hours, I'll empty almost the entire trailer and trade it for other goods. By the time I get the trailer unloaded, word has spread, and people come to trade goods, but it takes a while. Longer than any of the last couple of stops, that's for sure."

Linc nodded but said nothing. He would have to stay in the cabin the whole time and out of sight. That meant he couldn't move around that much.

After they finished breakfast, Jessi climbed back in the driver's seat. Linc laid down on the bottom bunk, grabbing a book. He was in the middle of a gay romance. He settled down to read about two men named Danny and Liam as they fought for a second chance at love.

Jessi drove a few more minutes before pulling into an old farmers market. There were already other sellers around with goods. Colorado Springs, surprisingly was populated for such a sizable pre-apocalypse town. Most people moved out of the large cities to get away from the sickness that took most of their loved ones. But Colorado Springs locked down their borders and wouldn't let people in. If people left, they weren't allowed to return. This gave them one of the highest survival rates in the entire country.

Jessi usually left here with a full truck that he could take and trade out for weeks. Even if he didn't have enough to trade, Iggy sent him with ten grand in cash, so he could buy what he couldn't barter. The money usually fluctuated, going up and down as he traveled.

He pulled up to an empty spot, checked to make sure Linc's door was locked. Then climbed out, closing the driver's door behind him. He lowered the lift and climbed on. Halfway through unloading his goods, he heard a commotion. Several traders had already come over to trade with him or asked him for something that he hadn't unpacked yet.

He jumped out of the back of the truck, not wanting to wait for the lift to lower. Pain shot through his stump as he landed. "Fuck," he cried, but he took off towards the sound. The cab door was flung open. The window was broken. He heard a scream moments before he cleared the cab.

Linc was being stuffed into the trunk of a car. Jessi didn't think he just ran. As he got closer, he realized it was Harvey himself that had come after Linc this time. Harvey climbed in the car and took off before Jessi could reach the vehicle. Jessi ran after the car, but it was no use. He fell to his knees, screaming Linc's name. He failed his boy, promising to keep him safe, and he failed him.

"Get it," a male voice yelled.

Jessi looked over; it was one of the other vendors at the market who had bought from him earlier. He winced as he climbed to his feet. His stump ached furiously, but that wouldn't stop him. He climbed in the man's truck and slammed the door shut. The man took off after Harvey's car.

"Name's Steve," the man said with a deep southern drawl.

"Jessi," he replied.

"You mind telling me what's going on? Why I'm chasing this man?"

Jessi didn't want to talk about Linc's horrors. He felt it wasn't his story to tell. However, this man had dropped everything to help someone he didn't know, so Jessi had to tell him something.

"Linc, that's the boy shoved into the trunk. I found him a few weeks ago, half-dead on the side of the road. He wasn't awake. So, I took him, cleaned him up and dressed his wounds. When he woke up, he told me he had been running from his captor. Harvey Collins killed his parents when he was a teenager. He then kept him captive for the last six years, raping him repeatedly, trying to impregnate him."

"Oh fuck, I never did like Harvey, but I didn't know he was a monster."

Jessi grabbed onto the oh-shit bar as Steve turned a sharp corner. He saw Harvey's car up ahead. They were gaining on him for a few minutes. Harvey must have realized he was being followed through because he sped up.

"Neither did I. I had been trading with him for a few years, but I always went to his barn. His wife was so nice, how could she have knowingly helped that horrible man keep Linc prisoner?"

"I have no idea I never met his wife, didn't know he had one. Whenever he came to town, he was always looking for a hooker." Steve opened his window. He turned his head and spat out some of his chew before mumbling, "bastard," without slowing. When he was done, he rolled the Window up and floored it.

"You look like a man who knows how to use this," Steve said, pulling a shotgun from behind the back seat.

"Hell fucking yeah."

Steve was gaining on Harvey. They were swerving down the mountain road that led back to Utah. Harvey had to know that Jessi would come after Linc, or maybe he didn't. Either way, Jessi rolled down the passenger side window once Steve pulled up to the side of Harvey's car.

Jessi cocked the shotgun and aimed at the tires. He didn't want to take Harvey out until after they stopped the car. He missed both shots and reloaded the shotgun with the shells that Steve had placed on the bench.

"Hang on," Steve yelled, slamming on the breaks. Jessi instinctively reached for the oh-shit bar again.

Harvey tore past them. Steve hit the gas and fell in behind Harvey's car. Both cars started taking the turns quickly. Jessi ripped the seatbelt across his chest in case they crashed. They followed Harvey for another fifteen minutes before the road straightened out

again.
"You ready?" Steve asked.
"Yeah, get me close."

Chapter 7

Linc had been reading the romance novel for a few hours now. He wasn't a significantly faster reader since he had no formal education. However, since he didn't have that much to do in Harvey's custody, he had gotten better. He was three-quarters of the way done with the book he had been reading. Liam and Danny were chasing their enemy through the city of Paris.

Just as Linc thought they were going to get Eclipse, they attacked Liam. The weird thing was he heard glass breaking at the same moment. The sound startled him, and he jumped. He hit his head on the top bunk from the fright.

When he looked towards the sound, his worst nightmare was in front of him. Harvey had found him. He screamed, "Jessi!" but Harvey's nasty hand clamped down over his mouth. The man pulled him out of bed roughly and twisted his hand behind his back so hard he screamed out in pain.

Harvey slipped restraints over Linc's wrists. The zip ties cut deep into Linc's skin as the mad man tightened them. "If I had time, I'd fuck you into submission right here, boy," he hissed.

Linc whimpered and breathed through his mouth, so he wouldn't have to smell Harvey's horrid stink. That was until Harvey slapped duct tape over his mouth. The man dragged him from the cab and across the parking lot. Linc fought and struggled as best he could, trying to slow Harvey.

Jessi was calling out from behind him. Linc smiled against the duct tape. But they still made it to Harvey's car before Jessi could reach them.

Linc stomped on Harvey's foot as hard as he could, but it was useless. Harvey still shoved him into the trunk and slammed it shut. He wiggled around a bit as the car started. His stomach lurched when the car started flying away from the one man who had protected him.

Jessi had always been so gentle with him. He called him kitten and bathed him. Linc realized that he was falling for the kind man. As much as he wanted nothing to do with relationships or sex, he couldn't help his feelings for the gentle giant.

He knew that Jessi would come for him, but he didn't know what would happen between now and then. What if Jessi didn't find him until after Harvey hurt him or worse? What if Harvey was taking him somewhere new that Jessi didn't know? Harvey's men had told him whom Linc was saved by, so he would know that keeping Linc at his house wasn't safe for Harvey.

Linc hoped Harvey was a stupid idiot and took him back to the farmhouse he dreaded. But he didn't think Harvey was that dumb. The man might not know that Jessi would come after them, but Linc didn't think Harvey would take the chance. He probably spent the last two weeks getting that bitch moved somewhere else. Then came after Linc.

Harvey could probably figure out most of Jessi's routes by calling his contacts. Jessi had hoped that by moving up his speed that Harvey would get to the cities too late. They hoped that Earl could take them out.

Linc had wanted no one killed, but he wouldn't even cry when Harvey took his last breath. He hoped he was there to see it and to smile in his face.

The car tossed Linc around the trunk as Harvey sped around the turns on the road that Jessi had come up a few hours ago. He didn't know how long he had been in the trunk lost in his thoughts. However, Linc knew the minute he was out of the trunk; he was going to vomit all his breakfast back up. He had already had to swallow some. Fucking tape.

He jumped out of his skin when a loud bang went off next to him, squeezing his eyes when he heard the sound. He knew that sound anywhere. It was a shotgun. His papa had taught him how to shoot when he was just a kid.

He squeezed his eyes closed again when another shot went off. The car was still speeding, and he didn't know if Harvey was doing the shooting or if Jessi had found them. He prayed for the latter.

The twists and turns started again, causing bile to rise in his throat as he was thrown across the trunk. After a few minutes, the turns stopped, and he heard the engine growl louder. Harvey was speeding up. The shots came a few seconds later, one right after another, then a third a minute later. Like whoever was shooting had to reload.

Linc didn't have time to think about that, though, because the third one hit one tire. He was suddenly rolling towards the left side. The car didn't slow. It sped up. But that gave Linc hope because that meant that Jessi was coming for him. Harvey couldn't drive long on a flat tire.

He heard another shot right before the car spun. Folding himself in half, he tried to brace himself as best as he could. He didn't know how many times the vehicle whirled in a circle, but it finally came to a stop.

Harvey's door opened; a second later, there were two rapid shots. Linc huddled in a ball waiting. Did Harvey kill Jessi? *Please let Harvey be dead,* he begged quietly.

The trunk popped open, Linc squeezed his eyes shut. He wanted one last second to believe that it was Jessi.

He whimpered when powerful arms wrapped around him and pulled him gently out of the trunk, "kitten, I've got you."

The boy opened his eyes; his handsome lumberjack was staring down at him. His eyes were full of concern. Not a scratch on him. "Harvey?" Linc squeaked out.

"Dead."

"Good," Linc said. He wrapped his arms around Jessi's neck and buried his face into the larger man's chest. Jessi carried him back to Steve's truck. The truck only had a front seat, so he climbed in with Linc still wrapped around him.

The driver drove off without bothering to say anything. They sat quietly in the truck's cab while Linc cried into Jessi's shirt. The larger man just rubbed Linc's back and comforted him as best as he could.

"Thank you for saving me," Linc said when he finished crying.

Jessi placed a soft kiss on Linc's forehead, "I will always take care of you, Linc."

Jessi shook Linc awake when they arrived back at Jessi's truck. Linc noticed that it was already almost dark when they got back.

"Fuck!" Jessi yelled.

Linc looked at what Jessi was looking at and saw there wasn't anything behind his trailer.

"Don't worry," Steve said. "They just packed your stuff up for you. I asked them before I jumped in my truck."

"Thanks, man," Jessi replied.

"Why don't you boys come down to my lady's diner and have a nice hot meal. Then you can have one room in the motel next door."

Jessi looked at Linc and raised his eyebrow in question. Linc smiled at the unvoiced question. Jessi was letting Linc choose what they were going to do.

"We would love too, um—" Linc paused when he realized he didn't know the man's name.

"Steve," the man supplied.

"We would love too, Steve, thank you."

"Great, we'll leave your rig here, I'll drive you back over in the morning."

Jessi nodded, and Steve took off down the road.

Chapter 8

Jessi carried Linc into the diner. Immediately, a short little older woman came running out of the back. She was plump and wore an apron, making her look like a wholesome southern grandma. She kissed Steve on the cheek and welcomed him home before turning to Jessi and Linc.

"Oh my, what in the dickens do we have here?" she questioned.

"Betty, this here is Linc and Jessi," Steve said as he walked behind the counter. He grabbed the coffee pot and poured two coffees. Walking over, he placed one down on the table across from the booth that Jessi settled Linc in. He put the second one down in front of Jessi. He returned to the back and brought out a glass of water for Linc.

"Oh yes, you come in a few times a year with a truck full of stuff. I remember."

"Yes, ma'am," Jessi replied. "And look at this poor thing, what happened?" she asked. She fluttered behind the counter, looking for something before anyone could answer. Yet, Steve spoke anyway.

"Harvey Collins came to town and tried to kidnap him."

She peaked up from where she was digging, "oh my, well bless your heart, sweet thing. I knew that man was bad news the moment I met him."

She came back around the counter with a first aid kit in her hands. Pulling a chair up from a table, she sat down in front of Linc. "Honey, can I clean you up?"

Linc looked over at Jessi, and Jessi nodded. Linc held out his wrists that were chaffed and bleeding from the zip ties placed around them. She cleaned the bloody areas and put the ointment over the wounds after wrapping both wrists in bandages.

"There you go, sweetheart." She handed Jessi bandages and the ointment. "Apply the ointment twice a day until the chaffing clears. Put new wraps on at least once a day."

Jessi nodded, "yes, ma'am. Thank you."

"No thanks needed. Now let me get you to something warm to eat. Will stew be okay, or I can cook up something else if that won't do."

"Stew is fine, ma'am. Right Linc?" Jessi responded.

"Yes, it's perfect. Thank you."

Betty carried herself into the back and came back a few minutes later with two bowls. She sat them down in front of Jessi and Linc before running off again. She wasn't gone for longer than a minute before she returned with two more bowls, some crackers, and rolls.

When she returned, she sat one bowl in front of Steve. She sat another across from him before placing crackers and rolls on the table.

Linc took a tentative bite and moaned. The sound went straight to Jessi's cock. *God, he was so gorgeous,* Jessi thought. He discreetly adjusted himself before digging into his food himself. Linc was right to moan. This was the best stew he'd had in a while. The four of them sat there, eating their stew quietly.

After they finished, Linc looked like he was about to fall asleep. Steve stood, "let me show you to a room."

Jessi looked at his boy, "do you want to walk?" Jessi would carry Linc any time. Even though his stump was killing him from all the activity that day, he would still do anything for Linc.

Linc stood and nodded. They followed Steve to a clean motel room. It only had one bed, but that was okay because Linc hadn't wanted to sleep alone. They both stripped down to their boxers and climbed into the bed. Jessi pulled Linc into his arms and said, "rest, kitten, I've got you."

It only took minutes for Linc to fall asleep, but Jessi laid there for a few hours. His brain wouldn't shut off. Everything inside of him wanted to drive nonstop back to the Yakuza territory and hide Linc away. But the other part of him knew his little town was counting on him delivering the goods he gathered.

逃走中

Jessi woke when Linc's lips touched his cheek, "good morning, kitten," he mumbled with a smile.

Linc leaned back and smiled back at him. "Good morning, thank you for saving me yesterday."

"Sweetheart, I need no thanks. I will protect you always."

Linc snuggled into Jessi's chest. After a few minutes of companionable silence, Linc asked, "Jessi?"

"Yeah, kitten?"

"I've um, I've never had an actual kiss. Um—will you, will you kiss me?"

Jessi lifted Linc's face gently, so he could look him in the eyes, "if you're sure that's what you want." He saw Linc's Adam's apple bob before he nodded. Jessi slowly leaned in to press his lips against Linc's. He went slow enough that Linc could pull away if he wanted.

With a sudden jerk, though, Linc closed the distance and pressed their lips together. It was closed-mouthed, but it was perfect.

Linc wrapped his arms around Jessi's neck and pulled himself closer to the larger man. After a minute, Linc's lips parted, and his tongue swiped across Jessi's bottom lip. Jessi to the hint and opened his mouth. Linc's tongue cautiously prodded his mouth, searching. Jessi carefully swiped his tongue against Linc's. His boy moaned.

Linc continued to explore Jessi's mouth. Soon Jessi was on his back with Linc on top of him. He let Linc control everything. The kiss was exploratory and inexperienced. Jessi's member rubbed against Linc's crack, and Linc gently rocked against the larger man.

Jessi could feel Linc's own cock rub against his stomach. "Fuck," he gasped when Linc pulled away.

Linc froze and looked down at Jessi. He stuttered, "is-is this, okay?"

Jessi's smile softened. He cupped Linc's cheek, "it's perfect, sweetheart."

Linc leaned back down and started pressing kisses to Jessi again. He pressed a kiss to his jaw, Adam's apple, chin, and then nose before he pressed his lips back to Jessi's. The whole while, he rocked against Jessi and moaned out his pleasure.

They were in nothing but their boxers, but Jessi didn't care. He would let Linc do whatever he wanted. If this was all Linc ever wanted, it was enough. It would always be enough. "Linc, sweetheart. I'm going to come."

Linc didn't pull away. Instead, his rocking sped up, and his kisses got sloppier. "Jessi!" he cried out a moment later. Jessi could feel Linc's release soak through the thin boxers he was wearing. The thought of getting to taste that sweet release had him following Linc in sweet harmony.

He grunted against Linc's lips while his orgasm pumped out of his dick. When he opened his eyes, Linc was straddling him, staring down at him in awe, "I never knew it could be that good. Did-did you like it?" he stuttered again.

"Sweetheart, it was perfect."

Jessi pulled Linc down to him, not caring about the mess in his boxers. He could deal with that later. He ran his fingers through Linc's hair until his boy fell asleep.

Chapter 9

It had lifted a weight off Linc's shoulders when Harvey died. The trunk ride had been scarier than hell, and he didn't want to leave Jessi's side. But when Jessi let him kiss him and then laid there letting Linc have all the control, he felt like he was finally free.

He wasn't sure if he could ever love Jessi enough. He hated himself for toying with Jessi's emotions, but he couldn't help himself. Jessi never once asked him to stop or started anything.

They had been on the road for weeks. Jessi was running his route as fast as he could. Generally, Jessi would rest overnight in the larger cities since they were safer. That way, he could rest his stump for a while. However, he wanted to get Linc back to the Yakuza, so he could see a doctor and to keep him safe.

Linc didn't mind one bit. He loved traveling with Jessi, learning so much from the stoic man already. At first, Jessi was silent, but soon Linc had him talking. Linc learned about Jessi's restaurant and his husband.

He felt Jessi's sorrow when he talked about his dead husband. But he also realized that Jessi's burdened shoulders seemed to get lighter the more he opened up to Linc. Linc had a feeling that Jessi hadn't opened up in a long time to anyone, probably not even his husband.

Jessi had shown Linc a picture of Geoff and him years ago while they had been on vacation. He had similar features to Linc but was closer to Jessi's age. They seemed very happy. Linc was torn; he wasn't sure what to do with that.

Every night, they climbed into bed together. He still didn't understand how the heck the giant lumberjack fit on the small bunk with Linc, but Jessi never complained.

The enormous teddy bear would hold Linc and kiss the back of his neck and forehead until Linc fell asleep. Sometimes Linc would kiss his lips, but it never got as far as that night in the motel room again. Linc was happy that Jessi wasn't pushing him and sad that Jessi didn't want him enough to persuade him.

The past four weeks had passed in a blur. They left Colorado Springs two days after they had killed Harvey. True to Steve's word, all of Jessi's goods had been put back on the truck. Someone had even fixed his window the next day. It didn't even take them a day to get to Denver.

After that, they never stayed over in towns. They would park at least a few miles outside of a city to sleep if they needed it. Jessi had cut off about half his travel time by not lingering in cities, but he seemed determined.

While they were driving, they would listen to music, or Linc would read aloud to Jessi. Other times Jessi would teach Linc how to operate the truck. That was Linc's favorite part, mostly because it allowed Jessi to take his foot off and give his stump a break.

Jessi thought he was hiding the pain from Linc, but Linc knew how bad the stump was hurting him. Linc didn't think it should hurt him that bad. His memory the first week he was with Jessi was hazy since he had still been in so much pain himself. But he was sure Jessi didn't hurt as much before Harvey's first attempt to kidnap Linc again.

Linc lost count of the number of stops they made along the way. Eventually, they ended up in Norfolk, VA, before they turned around and headed back west. Jessi dropped into North Carolina and took the I-40 for a little way to a small mountain town. They dropped off the fresh produce when they got there before getting back in the truck.

Jessi surprised Linc by only traveling a few miles before pulling in front of a gorgeous log cabin. He parked and turned the rig off, "come on; we're staying here for the night."

"We are?"

"Yeah, Joseph, back in town said an early snowstorm was coming in, and it wasn't safe to drive the roads at night. We might have to stay for two nights."

"But, it's only September?"

Jessi shrugged, "yeah, but it's the mountains they get snow year three-quarters of the year." Jessi climbed out of the cab, Linc followed. The moment his door was opened, he shivered.

Jessi was at his side before he could take a step. "Careful, there's already ice on the ground." Linc noticed that Jessi had a backpack in his hand and assumed a change of clothes was in it. "Let's get you inside before you freeze," Jessi added.

Linc didn't waste any time; he walked carefully in front of Jessi to the door. "Do I knock?" he asked. He didn't see any lights on inside, but he didn't want to barge in.

"No, it's empty; Joseph said he turned on the heater this morning when he heard we were on our way. So it should be warm, but no one's there."

Linc smiled; it seemed that Jessi had friends in every town he went. He probably had someone call ahead from their last stop earlier that morning when Linc was in the cab.

Ever since the kidnapping, Linc had been afraid to leave the cab unless Jessi was by his side. So when Jessi was unloading or loading things, he stayed hidden in the cab and read a book.

He opened the door, and a rush of warm air hit him. Flipping the switch, he hoped there was electricity, so he was happy when the overhead lights came on. The cabin was one enormous great room with a kitchen off to the side and a staircase that led to a loft.

He could see a giant bed sitting in the loft. There were two couches in the living room and two bean-bag chairs. The fireplace was crackling, heating the room. "Wow, it's beautiful."

"Yeah, it is, I usually stay here a day or two when I visit. This is my cabin, Linc. I owned it before the world went to shit."

"So, you and Geoff came here?"

The light in Jessi's eyes melted away as he thought about his dead husband.

"I'm sorry, Jessi, I didn't mean to—" Linc didn't know how to comfort the man. So he just wrapped his arms around Jessi's waist and laid his head against his heart.

"It's okay, Linc, it was a long time ago. And yes, we came here, it was our home away from home."

Linc pressed a kiss to Jessi's heart. "You were going to stop here regardless of if there was a snowstorm, huh?"

"Yeah," Jessi sighed, wrapping his arms around the smaller man.

They stood there in silence for a few minutes, just basking in each other's presence.

"Joseph's said he put the food in the fridge for us," Jessi said, pulling away from Linc. "Let's make dinner." They pulled apart. Jessi dropped the bag he was holding by the door and walked towards the kitchen, and Linc followed.

They found some deer steaks, potatoes and green beans in the pantry. Jessi went outside and started the barbecue. Then, he seasoned the steaks before putting them back in the refrigerator.

Linc peeled the potatoes, cut them and put them on the stove to boil. The two of them sat down at the table and snapped the fresh green beans.

They worked in companionable silence with gentle touches here and there. Linc was in heaven. He wished they could stay here forever. He rubbed his growing stomach. Even though he wasn't that large yet, he was almost five months along now. He assumed it was because the first three months he had been malnourished.

Jessi was doing an outstanding job of making sure he ate enough and drank enough. Linc wasn't used to eating when he felt like it or when he was hungry, so he would often forget.

"Hey, where'd you just go?" Jessi asked, placing his hand on top of Linc's.

"Just thinking how much I already love this place. It's beautiful here. So peaceful." Linc squeezed Jessi's hand.

Jessi's face lit up with one of the brightest smiles Linc had seen on the man. "I'm so glad you love my home, Linc."

"Can I ask you a question?"

"Always, but let me get these steaks on quick. Can you start the green beans?"

Linc nodded and stood with the colander of green beans. He walked over to the sink and rinsed them off before putting them in a pan to boil. He then checked on the potatoes; they weren't done yet, so he placed the lid back on them.

"So, what did you want to ask me?" Jessi asked. When Linc turned around, Jessi leaned against the sliding door that led to a deck and grill.

"I was just wondering why you don't just live here if you own this place."

"Geoff and I talked about it before the government failed after I lost my restaurant. This place was paid off, so we could have lived off the land here. But we wanted to help people. So, we sold our house on Long Island and bought my truck. After he died, I thought about coming back here and living out the rest of my days. But then Geoff would have died in vain."

Linc understood how Jessi felt. His family died in vain because that damn bastard wanted to use Jessi as a baby maker. Linc was equal parts pissed and happy that his body didn't cooperate, and it took five years before he got pregnant. In the back of his mind, he knew if he hadn't gotten away before the child was born, he would have never left.

Linc brushed a tear from Jessi's cheek before leaning up and pressing a kiss to the corner of his mouth. "I'm sorry you had to go through that." He pressed another kiss to Jessi's lips and wrapped his arms around Jessi's neck. Before they could get too far, the smell of char hit their noses.

"Fuck! The steaks," Jessi said, pulling away from Linc. He opened the barbecue to reveal smoking steaks. He flipped them over and closed the lid.

Linc rushed over to the potatoes and green beans. He poked the green beans. They had softened a bit and were just right, so he turned them off and dumped them into the strainer. Next, he tested the potatoes. They, too, were done, so he strained them as well after he dumped the strained beans back into the pan.

He added milk and butter to the empty pan to warm up and then seasoned the green beans. Jessi had a hand mixer, so he dumped the cooked potatoes back in the pot. As Linc was mashing the potatoes, Jessi returned with the steaks.

"They're a little charred and on the well-done side, which is probably better for you and the baby."

Jessi plated up the steaks and green beans. Linc plopped two servings of mashed potatoes on the plates before they sat.

"What do you mean?"

"Well, when I was training to be a chef, they teach you how to prepare all types of meat safely. They also teach you about cooking for people with medical conditions. Pregnant people, in general, shouldn't eat venison. But since we have nothing else."

Linc blanched, "maybe I should just get the potatoes and green beans."

"No, you need protein. I know little about pregnancy, but I know you need to eat a healthy diet."

They dug into their food after that, having a light conversation, but mostly, they ate quietly. When Linc and Jessi were done, they both washed and dried the dishes.

"You look exhausted. We should get you cleaned up and in bed," Jessi said. "The bathroom is upstairs."

Linc turned towards the stairs and was halfway up before he turned. "Jessi?"

"Yeah, kitten?"

"Will you—um," he twisted his hands together, looking nervous.

Jessi started across the room and up the stairs. He reached Linc and grabbed his hands. "What do you want, sweetheart?"

Linc loved all the pet names that Jessi called him. It made him feel special. "I was wondering if you'd like to um, join me?"

Jessi's eyes glanced down to Linc's lips, causing Linc to lick them unconsciously. Linc could see the want swirling in the other man's eyes, but Jessi didn't move.

Since Jessi was a step below him, he didn't have to stand on his tiptoes. He pulled Jessi's arms around him and then released his hands before wrapping them around Jessi's neck. He pressed a closed-mouth kiss to Jessi's lips.

"Please," Linc begged. He pressed another kiss to his lips, but this time, he waited for Jessi to return it. When he did, Linc ran his tongue across the seam in Jessi's lips. They both groaned when Jessi opened his mouth.

Jessi pulled his boy towards him and kissed him hungrily. "Linc," he pleaded.

Linc pulled away and led the lumberjack up the stairs and into the bathroom. He turned the water on before stripping down to nothing. "Well, are you just going to stand there or are you going to join me?"

Chapter 10

It conflicted Jessi. On the one hand, there was a gorgeous omega climbing into his shower, who seemed to know exactly what he wanted. However, on the other hand, could Jessi trust that Linc knew what he wanted? What if Linc was experiencing some rescue hero worship or something? Was he trying to give Jessi what he thought Jessi wanted?

The sexy little minx was driving Jessi bat shit crazy, that was for sure. But no matter how hot and cold the man was, Jessi knew he would wait as long as it took. He wanted his perfect little omega to trust him enough to allow Jessi to love him.

The lumberjack brushed a hand over his scruffy beard and sighed. He went to the bedroom and stripped since he was too large to be striping in the bathroom. He tossed his discarded clothes in the hamper before waltzing into the bathroom.

His little omega had already turned the hot water on and was making quite the scene for Jessi. His member hardened in seconds as the young man rocked his hips back and forth to the music in his head. He shimmied out of his pants at the same time.

He groaned with Linc turned. The little flirt was smirking. He knew what he was doing to Jessi. The man's eyes raked over Jessi's massive body, locking in on his gigantic cock. Jessi smirked. "You like what you see, kitten?"

Linc licked his lips and nodded. His cheeks pinked when his eyes met Jessi's, "Is that alright?"

Jessi stocked over to Linc slowly, never taking his eyes off the younger man. He was hungry, hungrier than he had been at dinner time. Only this time, he wanted to devour the skittish boy in front of him.

His boy glowed. He looked so much healthier than he had only a few weeks ago when Jessi found him on the side of the road. He stopped in front of Linc and ran his finger across the boy's face. "Are you sure you want this?" he asked.

"I-I," he stuttered. Linc dropped his gaze and didn't finish. He started crying.

Jessi pulled the young man into his arms, "oh, kitten. Ssh, now. You're safe." Jessi scooped the boy up and walked over to the bed. Linc sobbed on his chest. The whole time Jessi held him whispering nonsense to him.

After a while, Linc pulled away, "I'm sorry." Linc stuttered out.

Jessi lifted his hand to Linc's cheek and wiped the tears away. "Sweetheart. There's nothing for you to be sorry for, you hear me? You were kidnapped and raped repeatedly for years. You have every right to feel the way you do."

"You-you don't think I'm brok-broken?"

Jessi pulled Linc back to his chest and wrapped his arms around the boy. "Kitten, you are not broken. You are strong and brave."

"But-but, I can't—" he bawled.

"Ssh, it's okay. Let it out. I'm here. I will always be here."

"Jessi?" Linc whispered after a few minutes. He was sniffling, but his tears were drying.

"Yeah, Linc?"

"I want to, I really do."

"I know, sweetheart. When you're ready, I'll be here."

"What if I'm never ready?" Linc said into Jessi's chest.

"I'll be here," Jessi said simply.

"I don't deserve you," Linc whispered.

Jessi pulled back so he could look into Linc's eyes. He brushed Linc's long hair out of his face. "No, sweetheart, you are worth everything. You deserve to live your life free. The way you want. You are precious and beautiful. You're perfect in every way, and I will spend the rest of my days making sure you know that."

Linc smiled. It didn't reach his eyes, but it was true. He pressed a small kiss to Jessi's forehead. "Um, can we maybe, um cover up?" Linc asked, turning pink.

Jessi looked down and realized they were both still naked. "Oh, yeah, um. Why don't you take your shower? I'll, uh, throw pants on and take one after you."

Linc ran off to the bathroom with beautiful pink cheeks. As soon as the door was closed, Jessi sighed and flopped backward on the bed. He laid there for a few minutes, lost in thought before pulling his pants back on. "Geoff, what am I going to do?" Jessi groaned. He sometimes talked to his dead husband when he was lost.

But he meant what he said to Linc. He was already invested in Linc and was falling hard for the young man despite his better judgment. He would take care of him until Linc sent him away. If that meant living with blue balls for the rest of his life, so be it.

Once he had his pants back on, he dropped back on the side of the bed. Linc didn't take long to finish his shower. He came out of the bathroom with pajama bottoms on. Linc wasn't muscular by any means, but Jessi could still see the outline of his chest and arm muscles.

He was drying his hair out with the towel. When he finished, he looked up to see Jessi watching him. He blushed. "Um, sorry about earlier."

"Nothing to be sorry for, okay?"

Linc looked away and sighed. "Jessi, I want this. I want you. I-I—" he sighed again and dropped on the bed next to the larger man.

Jessi didn't reach for him even though he wanted to. But he squeezed Linc's thigh, "I know, kitten, and I'll be here when you're ready, okay?"

Linc nodded. And Jessi knew. He could see the want in Linc's eyes when he let himself go. He could it in the way Linc looked at him when he didn't think Jessi was looking.

"I'm going to go take a shower," Jessi said. "You look exhausted, let's get you into bed. Okay?"

Linc nodded again. Jessi helped him stand up, and he got the covers pulled back. He kissed Linc on the forehead after tucking the covers up under his chin.

"Goodnight, Linc."

"Goodnight, Jessi."

Jessi turned out the lamp next to the bed and made the way quietly to the bathroom. He sat on the toilet and took his leg off. He sighed when he saw how red and swollen the stump was. Thank goodness he had crutches in the closet. He figured that he would leave it off for the rest of the time they were here.

Maybe they could stay an extra day. After all, they were early. They could stay a week here and still make it back to the Yakuza early. In fact, the longer Jessi thought about it, the more he wanted to do it. He didn't have any perishables in the truck. So he didn't have to worry about getting to the next city, and Linc seemed to like it here.

He decided he would ask Linc tomorrow. He stood up and

hopped into the shower. Situating himself on the chair, turned the water on. He sat the chair, so his back was facing the showerhead. He leaned back into the spray and moaned when the warm water fell over him.

His cock grew as he thought about the young man in his care. He wished one day Linc would trust him enough to let him slip dip inside of his body and make him sing. He doubted that Linc had ever had consensual sex. He wanted very much to be the man that showed him how great sex could be.

Jessi scooted his chair, so he was leaning against the shower wall and took himself in his hand. He started stroking himself slowly. He imagined Linc at his feet. His arms wrapped protectively around his baby bump as he slowly sucked Jessi's member into his mouth.

"That's it," Jessi muttered. "Right there." He twisted his hand slightly when he reached his cock head before stroking back down. After a minute, he reached down with his other hand and grabbed his balls. Rolling them in his hand, pretending they were Linc's soft hands instead of his own. His strokes quickened as his fantasy continued.

The fantasy Linc winked wickedly at him as he stuck two fingers in his mouth. They were a slobbery mess when he pulled them out with a pop. He ran his hand under Jessi's balls and along his taint. He then rubbed the slobbery fingers in a circle around Jessi's hole.

Linc dipped one finger into Jessi's entrance. Jessi whispered Linc's name like a prayer as he furiously stroked himself lost in his fantasy. Linc's nose nuzzled his pubic hairs when he sucked Jessi all the way down. Jessi's hand tightened as he pulsed, thinking about how tight Linc's throat would be around his member.

Jessi didn't realize he was coming until his release struck him in the chest, pulling him from the fantasy. He cursed and let his head fall against the shower. He closed his eyes as the aftershocks from the orgasm racked his body.

Chapter 11

Linc hadn't fallen asleep as soon as Jessi tucked him in. He laid, staring at the ceiling in the dark. So, he heard Jessi in the shower. He listened to his name fall from Jessi's lips like a prayer. He wanted more than anything to go in there and be the only one making Jessi moan like that.

But he knew it was only happening in whatever fantasy that Jessi was having. Because Linc was a coward, he quietly tossed the blanket down to his feet and took his own cock in his hand. And started jerking it.

He imagined himself being brave enough to go into the bathroom with Jessi. What did Jessi imagine right now? Linc imagined sucking Jessi's massive dick into his mouth. He'd never given a blowjob in his life. But when he saw Jessi's weeping dick earlier tonight, he had wanted to.

Why was he such a coward? He had the man of his dreams literally standing there, lusting after him. But he couldn't go through with it. Tears spilled down his cheeks as he continued to jerk himself fastest.

He thought about how the water would sluice off his back while he sucked Jessi's cock all the way to the hilt. How his throat would constrict around the rigid member. Would he be able to take Jessi all the way? The thought of choking on the massive member had him speed up his strokes.

Linc strained to hear Jessi in the bathroom to enhance his fantasy of the man. The moans Jessi was making, even as faint as they were, had Linc to the brink of his orgasm. A loud curse followed by a thump had Linc spraying himself with his orgasm.

Minutes later, he heard the water shut off. *Shit! Shit! Shit!* He thought; he looked around and grabbed Jessi's discard shirt to wipe himself down quickly. He tossed the shirt back in the hamper and turned around to find Jessi staring at him. Jessi had his leg off and was using a pair of crutches.

His cheeks pinked when he realized he'd caught him red-handed.

"Linc? I thought you were going to sleep."

"Um, sorry. I ugh couldn't, um sleep. So, I was waiting for you."

"Oh, well, um you might want to um," Jessi said, waving one hand towards his bottom half.

Linc followed his line of sight and realized that his cock was hanging out of his pants still. "Fuck," he whispered and tucked himself back in. He felt his cheeks burning as he hurried around to his side of the bed.

Jessi said nothing though he just made his way to the bed.

逃走中

The next morning was awkward as fuck. Especially when Linc woke up wrapped around Jessi like an octopus. Jessi was already awake and running his hand lovingly up and down Linc's back.

"Morning," Linc mumbled into Jessi's chest.

"Morning, kitten." Jessi didn't stop his hands when he realized Linc had woken. They laid there quietly for a few minutes doing nothing.

"I, um, I need to pee," Linc said, breaking the silence. Jessi moved his arm and allowed Linc to scramble up. He went into the bathroom and slammed the door shut harder than he probably should have.

Last night after he crawled into bed, he faced the edge of the bed and scooched as far away from the man that he could. He was embarrassed by what he did last night and wasn't sure if he could face the man this morning.

He sighed and leaned up against the door. Jessi passed the bathroom door two minutes later, but Linc still didn't move. Jessi must have been on his crutches again because Linc noticed his leg still sitting next to the toilet.

His squished bladder called to him again, reminding him he needed to pee. He let out another sigh and did his business. He brushed his teeth with the new toothbrush that Jessi must have sat out for him the night before. After he was done, he went back to the loft and found one of Jessi's oversized t-shirts and slid it over his head.

He made his way down the stairs, where he found Jessi staring breakfast. He smiled weakly when Jessi looked over at him. His cheeks heated when Jessi smiled back. *Did Jessi know what I did last night?*

"You want some bacon, kitten?" Jessi asked.

Linc was sure he was only asking to start a conversation, so he nodded, "yes, please."

"There's orange juice in the fridge if you would like and some goat's milk. Joseph brought it over this morning, thought you would like some."

"Thanks," Linc mumbled. He walked past Jessi and opened the fridge. He grabbed the small container of orange juice out. When he turned around, Jessi was setting two glasses down.

"I'll take that, too."

Linc poured them both a glass of orange juice while Jessi went back to cooking. When he was done, he put the rest of the liquid back in the fridge.

Linc loved orange juice. It was one thing he regularly got when he was with Harvey. He grabbed his juice and sat down at the small table. It sat in the open space between the front door and the kitchen island.

After he finished, he watched Jessi finish plating their breakfast. Jessi tried to hobble over with one plate and one of his crutches. When Linc realized he needed help, he jumped to his feet and grabbed the plate from him.

"Sit, I'll get it."

Linc sat the plate down where Jessi would sit and went back to the kitchen for the rest of the food. He brought back the second plate, Jessi's juice, the salt and pepper, and Jessi's second crutch.

When he was done setting everything down, he sat down and smiled at Jessi, "sorry, I forgot you didn't have your leg on."

Jessi smiled back at him and placed his hand on top of Linc's. "It's alright. I've lived without a leg for twenty years now. So, I've adapted. I can carry stuff around while I use my crutches."

"I know, but you shouldn't have too," Linc said, squeezing Jessi's hand before pulling it away.

Linc moaned around the biscuits and gravy as they dug into their food that tasted like heaven.

"Sorry," he muttered when he saw Jessi staring at him. He sat down his fork and reached for Jessi's hand. He wrapped both of his around the larger man's. "Jessi, I am uh. I'm sorry about last night too."

Jessi dropped his fork and placed his second hand over Linc's hand. "Sweetheart, it's fine. You have nothing to be sorry for." His eyes softened, and he watched Linc for a minute. He finally reached up and ran his hand across Linc's jawline. Linc leaned into the touch moaning from the contact. He wanted Jessi so severely. "When you're ready, whatever you want, whatever you decide. I'll be here."

Linc didn't know what to say to that, so he just nodded at the other man. They sat there for a few minutes before Linc came to his senses and pulled his hands away. All Linc had to do was let himself fall, and this wonderful man would take care of him. Maybe that's what he feared. Linc didn't know. What he knew was Jessi was breaking down his walls with each sweet thing he said.

Chapter 12

They stayed at Jessi's cabin for an entire week before they headed out. Jessi showed Linc around and introduced him to the handful of people who still lived there. But they mostly kept to themselves.

Linc was distant the day after they arrived. He started opening up when he realized Jessi didn't hold what happened the night before against him. They spent their days relaxing and reading. Jessi loved reading to Linc. They would cuddle and even have hot make-out sessions and heavy petting, but clothes hadn't come off again.

When Jessi had walked out of the bathroom that first night, he knew what Linc had done in the bed. He also knew that Linc had heard him in the shower, but neither one of them acknowledged it. While Linc was in the shower the second night, Jessi placed a pack of tissues on the nightstand.

That night when he was in the shower, he jerked himself off again, pretending that Linc was between his legs. Linc was in bed when he returned to the loft in his sleep shorts. He knew that Linc had jerked himself off as well as soon as he looked at the younger man because his face flushed in embarrassment.

Jessi just smiled and pulled Linc into his arms. Kissed his forehead and tried his best to go to sleep. They would stay up talking until one of them fell asleep first.

Every night after that, while they were in the cabin, they did the same thing. Jessi would jerk off in the shower. Knowing that Linc was in the other room jerking off to the sounds he made only made Jessi harder. By the end of the week, Linc no longer flushed when Jessi came into the room afterward.

Each morning Jessi woke up with Linc clinging to him like Jessi was his own personal life raft. Jessi loved the younger man holding him like that.

They spent a week traveling through Tennessee and into Arkansas. They slept in the rig's cab curled around each other each night. Jessi started teaching Linc to drive during the long stretches of roads.

They didn't stop overnight in a town again until they got to Little Rock. Little Rock was like Colorado Springs with the open market where Jessi could park, sell, or trade. The day before, they had filled up on a bunch of produce.

Jessi pulled up in front of a motel at the end of the day and parked. The town gave him a free room whenever he was in town since he brought produce in. Everyone loved Jessi; it seemed.

"Alright, kitten. You ready?"

"He's truly dead, right?" Linc asked before he opened the door.

Linc hadn't seen Harvey's body himself since Jessi didn't want to subject the man to that. "Yes, sweetheart. I swear to you the man is dead. I checked his pulse myself."

Linc nodded and climbed out of the truck. Jessi walked around the cab with a bag in one hand and his crutches in the other. His stump was no longer sore after the blessed week at the cabin. At Linc's insistence, he took it off more often to allow his stump to keep from getting inflamed again.

Once they got to the room, Jessi sank on the bed and instantaneously pulled his leg off. Linc went into the bathroom and started the shower. "Hey Jessi," Linc called out.

"Yeah, kitten?"

"I'm um. I'm going to have to help you in the shower. There's no handicapped rail or anything." He noticed Linc looked nervous. He didn't blame him since neither had seen each other naked since the first night at the cabin.

While they had both jerked off and known, they were jerking off together. This was different because they were going to be naked in the small tub together.

They had stopped and taken a shower at a truck stop earlier in the week. But there had been a handicapped stall, so Jessi had needed no help.

"I can just take a bath, Linc." Any he could but—"You don't like baths. Let's get you in the shower."

Jessi nodded and stripped out of his clothes. He turned his back to Linc so he wouldn't embarrass the younger name. When he turned around, he was surprised to see that Linc had also stripped down to nothing.

He grabbed his crutches and made his way to the bathroom.

Linc followed him into the bathroom with no hesitation whatsoever. Jessi turned around and sat on the edge of the bathtub handing the other man the crutches.

Linc took them and leaned them against the sink, so they were out of the way before climbing into the shower. He blocked the water with his back and helped Jessi stand up, before shutting the shower curtain.

Jessi never enjoyed taking a shower while standing on his one leg unless he absolutely had too. He tried it once right after he lost his leg and fell. Luckily, his husband was in the other room and heard him hit his head. He ended up with a concussion from that experience.

Even with Geoff's help, he had only stood up in the shower a handful of times after that. This was one of those times.

"You good?" Lin asked after he got the curtain closed.

"Yeah."

Linc nodded. He turned and grabbed the removable shower head, and started rinsing Jessi off. "Just hold on to my shoulders, okay."

Jessi nodded. Linc could tell he was nervous. "I've got you," Linc promised. Kissing Jessi's cheek. After rinsing him off, Linc grabbed the shampoo and gently massaged the shampoo into his hair. Jessi moaned under his devotion; he couldn't help it. He felt his dick harden and bump against Linc's own hardened member, but he ignored it, and so did the younger man.

When Linc was done with his hair, he grabbed a washcloth. He quickly washed down the front of his body before having Jessi get his back.

Linc rinsed him off just as thoroughly and then shut the shower off to help Jessi out. "What about you?" Jessi asked.

"I'll finish up once you're out." Jessi could see understanding in Linc's eyes. The boy helped him sit back down on the edge of the tub and spin out. He helped him over to the toilet, where he could sit more stability and finish drying off. Linc moved his crutches so Jessi could reach them before returning to shower himself.

The whole time Linc didn't say a word. Jessi dried off and slipped out of the bedroom. A few minutes later, Linc returned with only his towel wrapped around him. He dropped the towel and climbed into his side of the bed. He pulled the covers over him and then rolled over and faced Jessi.

Jessi watched him. Lust was swirling in his black eyes. Yet, Linc knew from experience with Jessi that he wouldn't do anything until Linc started it. With that in mind, Linc hesitantly scooted closer to the larger man. He lifted his bare leg and placed it over Jessi's stump.

"Kiss me," he pleaded.

Jessi wasted no time responding to the man. He pressed his lips to Linc's in a beautiful closed-mouthed kiss. Neither of them moved until Linc slid his tongue across Jessi's lips. Jessi opened his mouth at the request and pulled his boy towards him.

The swell of Linc's stomach pressed against his as they kissed. Linc's hands were in Jessi's hair, tugging on his head, trying to deepen the kiss. His unpracticed tongue fought with Jessi's for dominance. They both moaned.

Linc thrust wildly against Jessi, whimpering. "Please," he gasped out. "Please!"

"I've got you, kitten," Jessi responded adoringly. Jessi reached between them and wrapped his hand around Linc's cock. He observed Linc for any sign that he wanted to stop. But his brown eyes were blown out and almost black with lust.

Jessi leaned in and pressed his lips to Linc's again. This time slowly as he stroked Linc to completion. It didn't take long, Linc pulled away, "Jessi, please."

Jessi nibbled on Linc's shoulder and bit slightly in the soft spot near the clavicle. Linc bucked into his hand once more. Jessi felt the warmth of his release splash against his stomach.

He kissed Linc slowly as the man came down from his orgasm. In minutes the boy was out. Jessi pinched his own erection, forcing it to deflate. This was all for Linc, and he wouldn't be careless enough to jerk himself off.

When he was sure Linc was asleep, he slipped out of bed and wiped himself down with a washcloth. When he returned, Linc immediately curled into his side. He wrapped himself around the larger man.

Chapter 13

Jessi finished packing up the trailer. They were almost home. More than half of the stuff in the trailer now was meant for the Yakuza. He couldn't wait to show Linc the little house he had back in Yakuza territory. He loved his cabin in the Tennessee mountains, but there was no room for a baby there. But he had two bedrooms at home.

Linc was across the parking lot, trading with a woman for new pants. He was halfway through his pregnancy, and his tummy suddenly jumped out the last week. Linc must have felt his stare because he turned towards him and their eyes locked.

When Linc smiled, Jessi smiled back.

Jessi placed the lock on the trailer door and then headed to the cab. When he got there, he noticed that the sat phone he kept on him was beeping. Iggy must have called him. He grabbed his grooming kit and decided he would call Iggy back once they were on the road in a few minutes.

He walked up to Linc and pressed a kiss to his cheek. His boy smiled in return. "I'm going to go clean up and shave. Then we can get on the road, yeah?"

"I'll come with you; we were just finishing up."

Linc was waddling, so Jessi offered his arm, and Linc took it without hesitation. He had been speaking up more lately and coming into himself, Jessi couldn't be prouder.

After they finished in the bathroom, Jessi helped Linc into the cab and then climbed in after him. Jessi put his stuff in the back and grabbed the sat phone, placing it in the cupholder in the front.

"What's that?" Linc asked.

Jessi sometimes forgot that Linc grew up in the middle of nowhere without access to electronics. "It's a satellite phone. Iggy called while we were loading up. I'm going to call him back once we are out of town."

Linc laid down in the back. Jessi waited for him to nod off

before he pulled out. His omega was exhausted.

It only took them a few minutes to get on the open road. They were just leaving what was left of Albuquerque, so they had plenty of open road ahead of them. They had four more stops to make before they got back to Yakuza territory. But they had a few hours before their next stop and overnight rest.

Jessi turned on the cruise control and then waited thirty minutes before he called his boss. He didn't want to wake Linc up accidentally.

"Hello?" the voice of his boss Iggy said from the other end.

"Boss?" Jessi replied.

"Jessi, thank God."

Jessi's voice instantly changed to concern; he must have heard the worry in Iggy's voice. "What's wrong, Iggy?"

"When was the last time you got an update from someone?" he asked.

"Been a few months, last I heard was about your father's death."

Jessi heard someone mumble to Iggy before hearing footsteps leaving Iggy's side.

"Shane Lynch is dead, his son Declan killed him. Then he and his mother, Mia, fled into the night," Iggy said.

"Wow, that's good news, isn't it?"

"Yes, but that also means we don't know who is going to take over for the Irish. Will they be better or worse?"

"That's a good question. Why did his son run? I would have thought he would have just taken over. I heard he was just as ruthless as his father."

"Out of necessity only. Turn's out that Declan's an omega."

"Fuck!" Jessi spat. "How'd you find that out?"

"De and his mother are here."

"What?!" Jessi exclaimed.

"Jessi?" Linc called out softly.

Fuck! He covered the speaker with his hand and looked back and Linc, "sorry, Linc, I'm on the phone. You okay?"

"Yeah, I'm okay." Jessi turned back to the conversation, but a moment later, Linc came out of the cabin and sat in the passenger seat.

"Sorry about that, I picked up a passenger."

"I guess I'm not the only one that has a story to tell?" Iggy teased.

Jessi snorted, "no, I guess not. But tell me about this, Declan. Someone seems smitten." He reached over and pulled Linc's hand to his mouth and kissed it. *Sorry*, he mouthed.

Linc nodded and buckled up in the passenger seat.

"I'm in love with him, Jes. And he's pregnant."

"We'll shit a lot happened in a few months, didn't it?"

"Yeah, so we need to find an OB/GYN or a perinatologist."

"Well, shit, Iggy. I haven't run into any doctors that I know of."

"What about hospitals? Are any of them still opened?" Iggy replied.

"I'll start checking, but I was on my way home the trucks full, and I have a problem of my own."

"Which is?" Iggy prompted.

Jessi sighed, "I have a pregnant omega with me. His name is Linc. Iggy, he was being um... abused and um... raped. I need to get him to safety."

"Bring him here."

"That was the plan. I'm three days out."

"But that means you can't check for doctors," Iggy concluded.

"Right, I'm sorry, Iggy."

"No, your omega's safety is more important. Others can help look."

"I'll be there in three days, once I get unloaded, I can go back out again," Jessi said with a sigh. He didn't want to drop Linc off and leave him there, but if it meant finding a doctor for Linc and Declan, he would do it.

"Great thanks, man."

Jessi hung up the phone. He was happy for his friend Iggy, but now he wondered if the Yakuza would be a safe place for Linc and the baby.

He immediately pushed that thought away. The Yakuza had saved him when he and his husband was attacked. From what he could tell, they rescued a lot of other people. No, the Yakuza was the best place for Jessi to take Linc for the rest of his pregnancy.

"So, what was that about?" Linc asked after a few minutes.

"Sorry I woke you, kitten; I didn't mean too."

Linc waved him away, "it's fine. So?"

Jessi spent the next hour educating Linc on the recent history in and around San Francisco.

As a child, Linc's studies had included reading and writing what he needed to do farm work. Everything else was unimportant, according to his mother. Jessie explained how the Death Flu had killed everyone who caught the virus. For years, they had no cure everything they tried failed until they started mixing in the DNA from wolves.

Over seventy percent of the population died before a cure was even successful. Some crime syndicates took their members away from the cities and refused to let any sick people in. In the end, that saved many people, but for most, it was too late many of the large cities were half derelict.

Iggy's father, Takamori, had hidden his family, and the Yakuza, away on his estate outside of San Francisco. Eventually, building it into the small town it was today.

The Russians, Italians and Chinese also went underground. The Irish took over San Francisco. They drove out the Mexican street gangs and anyone who was not white, straight and alpha or beta. And they didn't stop there. People either joined Shane, fled, or were killed.

When Shane came barging into Yakuza territory, however, Takamori put his foot down. A war between them ensued until they killed Takamori and his son Kano.

"They killed them, just because they were like me?" Linc asked in a tiny voice.

Jessi had pulled off the side of the road a few minutes ago when Linc whimpered at Jessi's stories. "Oh, sweetheart. Come here."

Even at five months, pregnant Jessi could easily pull the young man into his arms. Linc wept for his fellow omegas that had fallen at the hands of the Irish.

Jessi wrapped his arms around Linc in return and kept him safe until he fell asleep. It was getting dark, so Jessi figured it was a good enough place for them to pull over for the night.

He gently lifted Linc and carried him to the back to lay him down before he started making dinner.

He would tell him about Shane Lynch killing Iggy's father and brother. Then Declan Lynch was escaping his father's grasp tomorrow.

Chapter 14

The stories that Jessi told Linc of the last couple of days had Linc shaking to his core. Why hadn't his parents ever told him what happened? Yeah, he knew there was some virus that had caused mass causalities. But he didn't know the extent, and he didn't realize that it killed over ninety percent of the world's population. That was just crazy.

No wonder most of the towns they drove through were barren and torn apart. While the ones they stopped in were barely functioning. It didn't surprise him now that they hadn't been able to find any doctors. From what he could tell, most doctors and nurses died fighting the viruses. The ones that were left were well protected by the people surrounding them.

Jessi pulled Linc from his thoughts as he pulled up to a small town. He stopped in front of the first houses. It looked like the streets weren't big enough for his truck to fit through. "We're home," Jessi said.

Linc looked out the front window and at the town. In the distance, he saw a wall that hid more homes. In the center of those homes was a massive estate.

All the homes except the massive estate looked like one to two-bedroom residences. There might even be a couple of three-bedroom dwellings. All of them were small and squished together, nothing like the ranches that he had grown up around.

Jessi opened the passenger side door and helped Linc out. He sat him down gently on the ground and kissed his cheek. There was already a crowd forming at the front of the truck.

"Jessi! Babe," a small Asian man called from a distance.

Jessi turned towards the voice with an enormous smile. The young man plowed into Jessi's arms as he was engulfed in a hug. "Toy," he said, kissing his forehead.

Linc wanted to rip them apart; Jessi was his. Damn it. The ash and sandalwood smells were his to roll around in no one else's. *Jeez, where had these possessive thoughts come from?* Linc thought to himself as Jessi pulled away from the other man.

The lumberjack pulled Linc into his side as soon as he was free and wrapped his arm around him. Linc rested his head on Jessi's chest. "Toy, this is Linc. Linc, this is my friend Toy, he and Kagiyama saved my life in San Francisco."

Oh, oh. The jealously that Linc was feeling drained his body. He reached out and took Toy's hand. "Thank you."

"Anyone would have done the same," the other man mumbled, blushing shyly. "Aren't you just so precious? Nice to meet you and welcome to Copperfalls." He said, kissing Linc's cheeks.

"Oh, we have a name now?" Jessi asked.

"Yeah, the town decided on it a few weeks ago."

"I like it," Jessi said. "I'm going to take Linc up to the main house and introduce him to Iggy, yeah?"

"That would be good. I'm sure that Declan will want to meet him too. He's been perfect for Iggy," Toy responded.

"Glad to hear. See you around, Toy."

Jessi pulled Linc with him up the street. There were people outside wondering about without a care in the world. Linc saw other people working and children playing. It was a perfect little town. Linc knew instantly that he would be happy here.

His lumberjack pointed out the temple and the market on the way to the gates. Jessi told him they didn't exchange money here, at least not at the moment.

Apparently, every who could have a job and they supported each other. They only used the money for outside transactions when needed. Everyone was feed and had a roof over their head.

Many people came up to Jessi and said hello as the two of them made their way through the streets of Copperfalls. Jessi kept Linc tucked into his side the whole time, somehow knowing that he was on edge and needed the comfort.

Linc was not used to this many people at all. He met more people in the last twenty minutes than he had his entire life. That included the people he met as he traveled with Jessi these previous couple of months.

The streets inside the walls were a bit more deserted than the ones outside the borders. The entire time they walked, people stopped them to introducing themselves.

There were two guards on either side of the two large doors

that sat at the front of the vast estate sided house. Linc had seen nothing like it. The doors were more extensive than average and sat side by side.

Both guards were large Asian men, alphas from the smell of them. One nodded to Jessi and Linc, while the other said, "Jessi," with a curt nod and opened the door.

An older Asian woman came walking in from another room, "Jessi-kun!" she called and pulled Jessi into a hug.

"Ms. Rei," he replied, hugging her back. When he pulled away from her, he immediately folded Linc back into his side. "Ms. Rei, this is Lincoln. Linc, this is Iggy's housekeeper and cook, Ms. Rei."

She patted Linc on the cheek before pulling him into her tiny frame. "Lincoln-kun," she said when they pulled apart. "Another baby, how wonderful. They are a blessing, especially now," she said in her broken English. "Come, Ichirou-san, want to see you now."

She turned on her heel and led the way down the hallway. Jessi and Linc followed behind, Jessi gripping Linc's shaking hand tightly.

"Wait here," Rei said before opening a door and walking inside.

Jessi kissed Linc on the forehead, "relax, kitten. These are good people."

"It's just there are so many of them."

Before Jessi could respond, the door opened back up.

"Kick off your shoes," Jessi whispered against Linc's ear. Linc did as Jessi asked.

"Jessi-san and Lincoln-san," Ms. Rei announced before leaving the room.

A small, tiny man, shorter than Linc, came over and pulled Jessi into a hug. Linc's jaw ticked until he realized that the smell coming from the man was all alpha. How could such a tiny man be an alpha? The man had a top know on his head and tattoos peeking out from under his clothes.

Linc turned his attention to the rest of the room. The room obviously was decorated with a woman's taste in mind. While the house looked all American and had the traditional doors, the décor in this room was different. There was a table about the height of a coffee table, but it was larger, almost like a dining room table. Around the table were several large cushions that seemed to sit directly on the floor. A wooden chair back was behind each pillow. There must have been a legless chair underneath the cushions. They covered the floor in straw mats.

Next to the empty cushion that Iggy just vacated was a larger man. He was brawny and had red hair, green eyes, and smiled fondly at Linc. Two older women were sitting on the other cushions. One was the Irish man's mother, with the same green eyes, and red/grayish curly hair. Her counterpart must have been Iggy's mother.

"Iggy, good to see you. Toy and his guys are unloading my truck as we speak. This is Linc."

"Linc, this is my boss, Ichirou, but everyone calls him Iggy."

Linc paled when Iggy went to shake his hand, so he pulled back and turned towards Declan. Declan was already up and wrapping his arms around Linc, who was now shaking, "ssh, it's okay. I promise none of the alphas here will hurt you. Why don't we go get you cleaned up, yeah?"

Declan's voice was soothing and had Linc relaxing into his arms. He sported his own baby bump, although it was smaller than Linc's. Declan looked over Linc's head to his boyfriend. Iggy nodded, and Declan pulled the terrified omega out of the room.

"Rei-chan, can you send for Toy please?" Linc was glad for it. He liked the other omega he had met earlier, as well. He didn't feel as overwhelmed as he did a few minutes ago. "Do you have your own clothes?"

Linc nodded, "in the truck."

"Rei-chan," he called.

"Yes, Declan-san?" the older housekeeper stopped and turned towards Declan.

"Please have Toy bring some of Linc's clothes. They are in Jessi's truck."

She nodded and turned back around. Declan led Linc through the house and up the stairs. "So, what was that room?" Linc asked curiously once he relaxed a bit.

Declan led him into a bedroom with a massive bed in the center. It smelled like Declan and the alpha, Iggy. "That is Hayashi's sitting room. She is Iggy's mother. The woman that was sitting next to her is my ma, Mia. Hayashi is from Japan. She keeps her sitting room set up like a traditional Japanese room called a *washitsu*. They cover the floors in mats called *tatami*. The Japanese sit on the floor in legless chairs called, *zaisu*."

"That's cool, but how do you get up off the floor with you know—" Linc asked, pointing towards Declan's baby bump.

Declan laughed, "I'm only three months along, I can still get up and down easily. I imagine that will change the further I get along."

"Yeah, I didn't start having issues until about a week ago."

Declan disappeared into the bathroom for a few minutes. He heard the water turn on, "let's get you in the bath, shall we?"

"That sounds wonderful, and I haven't had a bath since I was a kid."

"Well, then this will be a treat, huh?" Declan smiled.

A knock came at the door, "De, it's me."

"Come in, Toy."

The door opened and then closed. The young Asian man that Linc had met earlier came in with one of Jessi's bags. "I brought some of your clothes, Linc."

"Thank you."

"Come on, Toy, we're going to relax in the bath."

"What?!" Linc exclaimed, blushing.

Declan laughed and squeezed Linc's hand. "Relax, honey. The Japanese commonly bathe together. They have huge Jacuzzi-style bathtubs. Generally, Iggy and I don't share ours with anyone else. We go to the bathhouse instead sometimes to meet with Toy and some other friends. If you're uncomfortable, we can leave you too it, or we can wear underwear."

"It's normal?" Linc asked.

"Yeah, perfectly, it took me some time getting used to it, so I understand if you want your privacy."

Linc smiled, "thank you, but I think I would enjoy the company."

Toy jumped up off the bed, "alright, come on, girls; it's bath time."

The three of them walked into the bathroom. True to what Declan said, there was an enormous bathtub in the corner enough to fit several large men. They stripped out of their clothes, Declan helped Linc climb in the bath and settle. Almost as soon as they had settled, a knock came on the bedroom door before it opened.

"Declan-san?" Rei called out.

"We're in the bathroom, Rei-chan."

The older woman walked into the bathroom unashamed since they left the door open. She had a tray with food.

"I thought you boys would like some snacks," she said, setting the tray on the flat shelf like area on the side of the tub.

"Thank you, Rei-chan."

Once she left, Linc grabbed some crackers and started munching on them as he sighed into the bathtub. "What's the words I hear you saying after everyone's name?" Linc asked.

Declan explained the Japanese traditions of using san, chan, and kun as signs of respect. Then told Linc he didn't need to worry about doing it himself unless he wanted too.

The three of them relaxed and exchanged stories in the tub until they were wrinkly.

Chapter 15

Toy and Declan had brought Linc home refreshed and smiling. He had never looked so carefree like someone had lifted a weight off of him. Linc walked into Jessi's arms the minute that Jessi opened the door. His two new friends stood silently behind him.

Thank you. Jessi mouthed over Linc's shoulder as he settled into his arms. Linc buried his nose into Jessi's armpit and sighed. After a minute, he rested his head on Jessi's chest. "Declan said there weren't any empty houses for me to live in. I could stay with his ma, or many other people, or even their own house. But I told them I rather stay with you," he said. "I mean, if that's okay with you."

Jessi smiled down at his boy, "you can stay with me as long as you want."

"Really?"

"Yes, kitten. Wherever you want, would you like to see the house?"

Linc nodded eagerly. "Yes, please." He turned towards Declan and Toy. "Thanks for bringing me home. Would you mind showing me around tomorrow?"

Toy spoke up, "We would love too."

Linc pulled away and hugged both men before they turned and left. When they were gone, Jessi pulled Linc into their house, "I've got two bedrooms. Do you want—"

Linc cut him off by smashing his lips to the older man. When they pulled apart, they were both breathless. "Take me to bed, make love to me."

Jessi looked into Linc's eyes, studying them for a minute, "are you sure."

His boy nodded shyly and bit his bottom lip, "yes."

Jessi picked Linc up like he weighed nothing and walked down the hallway. Linc didn't have time to notice the bright kitchen or the warm living room as his lips were all over his man.

The lumberjack laid his boy out on the king-sized bed before removing his leg as quickly as possible. He grabbed the bottle of lube he kept in the bedside dresser before crawling over Linc. He hovered above the younger man for several minutes, just staring at him.

Linc squirmed under his gaze, "please," he begged. "I need you." Jessi smashed his lips to Linc, taking them in a deep passionate kiss. Pouring all of his love into the kiss, everything he couldn't say. Linc was his. He had been from the moment Jessi found him on the side of the road two months ago.

The burly man would do anything for the man underneath him and had. He killed his abuser and rescued him more than once. But Linc saved Jessi too. Before Linc appeared in his life, Jessi had been living on autopilot. Yes, it had only been a year since his Geoff died, but it had felt like an eternity and Jessi had been stuck, lost in limbo.

Linc whimpered and bucked up into Jessi, looking for friction on his hard cock. Jessi trailed kisses along Linc's jawline and his Adam's apple, smelling him. Linc smelled of delicious peaches. Jessi licked and nipped at his skin. He pulled back long enough to help Linc out of his shirt before his lips were back on the man.

He sucked in one of Linc's nipples making the boy arch up and gasp. "Please, Jessi! I need to touch you," he said, clawing at Jessi's shirt.

Jessi ripped his shirt over his head with one hand. "Fuck, sweetheart, you're so beautiful." He rubbed his hands lovingly over Linc's baby bump, kissing his way down to it.

Linc hands gripped Jessi's hair tightly as he tried to get friction on his achy cock. Even in his heats, he had never experienced this need to be with anyone. But he needed Jessi inside of him more than he needed his next breath.

He wasn't sure when it happened. One moment he was sitting in the tub with Declan and Toy, telling them about their incredible journey. And the next, he needed this sweet, sweet, patient man.

Jessi kissed the inside of his thigh then the other one, then licked one of his balls. Linc thought he would explode right then and there, but he didn't. Then Jessi's tongue licked a stripe from the base all the way to the tip. He circled and sucked the head of Linc's cock into his mouth.

Linc moaned. No one had ever cared about his pleasure, his

orgasms before. "Jessi! Oh, my God, I'm going too—" he didn't even finish before his release was exploding into Jessi's mouth. Jessi swallowed his cock as far as he could. Licking up every last drop of cum before letting Linc's cock slip out of his mouth with a lewd pop.

"Hold your legs up, sweetheart," Jessi said, pushing Linc's legs up. Linc did as he was told, trying to see what Jessi was going to do next over his baby bump. Jessi stuffed a pillow under Linc's ass, and then he was on him again. His mouth trailing kisses passed Linc's balls to his most private of areas.

"Jessi!" Linc screamed when Jessi's tongue licked around Linc's wrinkly entrance. His hole was perfect, Jessi thought. So pretty, he licked and licked until Linc relaxed under his ministration. "Fuck! Jessi, God, I'm gonna—"

"That's it, kitten. Come as many times as you need." He dove back in and stabbed his pointed tongue into Linc hole, spreading it opened. The muscles clenched around his tongue as Linc pulsed in Jessi's hand.

Jessi sped up his strokes on Linc's member as his tongue swirled, nipped, and licked at Linc fluttering hole. He felt Linc stiffening, so he used his free hand to rub a circle around his pink hole before push inside. The minute his finger popped through, Linc's dick pulsed and spewed.

"So good, please, Jessi. Now, need you," Linc repeated as Jessi continued to in his unrelenting attention to Linc's hole. His fingers stretched Linc until he had three fingers twisting alongside his tongue.

Jessi's cock was so hard one move, and he would spill his seed all over his bed. He pulled back with one last lick before climbing over Linc's stomach to kiss the man. Linc moaned into his mouth, his cock already hard again. "Please," his boy whimpered underneath him.

His hands worked to cover his cock in lube while he kissed the fuck out of his boy. When his cock bumped up against Linc's hole, he pulled away. "You're sure you want this."

Linc nodded, "you've been so patient with me, but if you don't get your dick inside of me now, I'm going to explode." His tone was crass, nothing like the sweet boy that he had fallen in love with. Yet he started pushing inside anyway, staring at his lover watching for any pain.

However, Linc was only smiling. He relaxed again once the

bulbous head of Jessi's cock popped inside. Jessi was huge, so he pushed in slowly. Linc's legs wrapped around Jessi's back, his hands grabbed onto Jessi's arms. His nails dug into the tattoos on his forearms.

When Linc's face screwed up tight, Jessi paused, pulled out a little, then pushed back and. Gently he rocked back and forth until he was seated completely. He smiled when his balls slapped obscenely against Linc's ass. He leaned over and pressed gentle kisses to Linc's lips. Linc returned the kisses hungrily, digging his claws deeper into Jessi's arms.

He pulled away, breathless, "please, move," Linc begged.

With one last kiss, Jessi pulled back slowly before slamming back in. He did that several times, making Linc squirm and moan. He was finally inside the hot little, sexy man, and he was going to show Linc just how perfect he was and how to be loved.

"More!" Linc demanded when he repeated to slide out slowly and then thrust back in.

Jessi started relentlessly pound into his little omega. The boy screamed and bucked and pushed back with every thrust. "Harder, please, Jessi, so good, fuck," he repeated over and over. He took his boy's lips in a brutal kiss as his balls tightened. Knowing he was about to spill inside this man, he wrapped his large hand around Linc's prick.

It only took two strokes before Linc was clamping down on Jessi's pulsing dick. Jessi yelled out himself spilling one of the best orgasms of his life inside the sweet, sweet boy.

Without thinking, Jessi's teeth found the soft spot of Linc's clavicle and bit down hard. He didn't mean to do it. He started freaking out when he tasted Linc's blood, but then Linc's teeth sunk into his neck in the same spot.

The shock he felt next was more than he ever thought possible. It was like he was hovering above his body, watching the mating below because that's what it was. They weren't having sex; they weren't even making love. They were mating. It was primal, raw, and perfect.

Jessi felt Linc's soft, fragrant soul mix with his and knew that they would forever be combined. His love for Geoff still was there locked away in a space in his heart just for that man. But the love he had for Linc was all-encompassing and new.

After what left like forever, he lifted his head and stared down into Linc's eyes, "I love you," the boy said with a smile.

Jessi smiled back; he ran a finger against Linc's cheek. Linc leaned into it without thinking. "I love you, too," he whispered, kissing Linc's lips softly. He still wasn't sure what happened, but a part of him knew that he and Linc would be forever connected. The more he thought about it, the more he loved it.

After a few minutes of watching each other in a daze, Jessi pulled away. Letting his softening cock slip out of his boy. He collapsed on one side of the bed and pulled Linc into his arms.

He kissed the back of Linc's neck. "Sleep, sweetheart."

Chapter 16

Shock went through his system when Jessi bit into his shoulder. However, before he could say anything, the rightness of it washed over him, and he returned the bite. Several days later, he still didn't know what that was about, but he felt connected to Jessi on a whole new level.

And the sex, oh my God, he had no idea sex was supposed to feel like that. When Harvey raped him, the man never touched Linc back or cared about Linc's comfort. His hole always burned for days afterward. Especially after a heat when it had been nonstop for a few days.

But with Jessi, it was like time stopped, and Linc was the most precious thing in the world. By the time Jessi slipped inside of him, everything was on fire in the right way.

Linc smiled against Jessi's warm body as the sunset in the distance. He had never enjoyed watching the sunset since his parents were killed. Having this with Jessi was a real blessing.

Linc was nodding off against Jessi's chest when they heard a commotion. "What the heck?" he asked Jessi sitting up.

"I don't know."

They both stood. Even though he had only been here a few days, he knew that this commotion was not expected. He could hear people shooting, men in particular. The two of them rushed through the house and out the front door. Guards were running by.

Jessi stopped one that Linc didn't recognize, "what's going on?"

The older Asian man responded, "they attacked the clinic." He pulled away and followed the other guards down the street.

Jessi turned towards Linc, "stay here. Lock the door."

Linc complied and ran inside. As soon as they locked the door, Jessi took off after the guards. When they got to the clinic, he saw a mess. There was a blood trail in the street, and Yori, the nurse, laid there with a wound in her abdomen. She was pale, but several people were helping her. There wasn't anything he could do. He looked around and saw that Mura, Iggy's *wakagashira,* was barking out orders.

He walked that way, "anything I can do to help?" he asked once the guards turned away from Mura.

"Is Linc safe?"

"Yeah, he locked himself in the house before I came over."

"Good, you know how to use this?" Mura asked, holding a gun up to Jessi.

He did, he didn't want too, but he could. He gulped and nodded. "Yeah, not by choice, but yeah." He carried a gun with him in the truck just in case. He only had to use it that one time in San Francisco when Geoff was killed. Not that it did any good.

"Good, the guards, are spread thin, take Tada and start searching each house. Start on the west side, check every nook and cranny."

Jessi turned to find the guard that he stopped earlier behind him. "Let's go."

He and Tada searched house to house for hours to no avail. They met up with other teams. But no one found any trace of the people that hurt the poor couple that happened to be seeing the doctor.

Luckily Yori was stabilized any was resting with Declan's mother in her extra bedroom.

Jessi returned to his house to find Linc curled up on the bed in a ball, shaking and crying.

"Sweetheart, what's wrong?" he asked, pulling his boy into his lap.

"I'm scared. What if they come again? And they kill more people."

Jessi tried to soothe Linc's worries. He rocked him and whispered sweet nothings into his ear until he fell asleep. After that, he laid awake for hours before he fell into a restless sleep.

逃走中

Linc was tired from the late-night, so Jessi left him to rest while he went to the market. He locked the doors to be on the safe side and headed out. He talked and caught up with a few people in town as he picked up what they would need for dinner.

A crowd started forming as cars drove up, and he knew Iggy was back in town. He pushed his way to the front of the group. Declan flanked Iggy, and a handful of people included Mura and another man he had never seen before. He was American, maybe Italian descent, he couldn't really tell from this angle.

He noticed that Dave Burns and Renzo Parra were standing side by side, blocking Iggy's path. They painted their faces in a scowl. "This is your fault," Dave voiced towards Declan loud enough for the crowd to hear him.

There were murmurs around the crowd, some in agreement, some not. Iggy stepped in front of Declan, followed by Mura, Hana, the new guy and Kagiyama. Toy reached for Declan's hand and squeezed it standing next to him. Toy whispered something to Declan, but Jessi couldn't make it out.

"You have a problem?" Iggy asked Dave and Renzo. Declan looked around to see if anyone else was joining behind the two, but there wasn't. Tada, the guard from the night before, and two other men also joined Iggy's entourage. Jessi pushed forward in case he needed to help.

"Yeah, you killed your own man over this outsider, this *Irish* man," Dave sneered. "Now we're being attacked because we are protecting someone who's not *kumi*. You no longer have the best interests of the Yakuza in mind. I challenge you, *oyabun*."

Iggy scoffed, "you? you're barely *kumi-in*."

"*Wakagashira!*"

"Yes, *oyabun?*" Mura replied.

"I banish these two men. Escort them out of town. Unless you rather perform *seppuku* for an honorable death?"

Jessi had followed most of the conversation up to that point. Even with the Japanese terms. He did not know what *seppuku* was, but he suspected it was a suicide ritual that samurais were famous for.

Both men glared at Iggy but realized they were out numbers, "fine, we'll leave."

"Mura, make sure you advise all the *kumi* that if we see them again, they should be brought to me immediately. Dead or alive," Iggy added without taking his eyes off the men.

"Yes, *oyabun*." Mura waved. Several men took Dave and Renzo into custody, escorting them out of sight.

"Listen up," Iggy yelled over the crowd. "Declan is to be my *otto,* which makes him *kumi.*" Iggy turned to Declan and whispered something before they turned around and left.

He knew *otto* meant husband. He had heard Iggy's mother call her husband that from time to time.

Turning, he headed back to his home, his shopping down. Linc should be awake now, so he couldn't wait to cuddle.

Chapter 17

The two men walked into the clinic. They had cleaned it up after the attack. The day after, they had escorted Dave and Renzo out of the town. Iggy announced that they had a new doctor. The man that came back with Iggy and Declan was an OB/GYN.

A week later, they were finally ready to reopen the clinic. Jessi was happy because he wanted Linc to get checked out. Linc seemed happy and all. He was healthy, glowed, and had gained weight. Jessi still wanted to make sure there were no lingering effects from Harvey's abuse. He also wanted to verify there were no complications from the pregnancy.

Yori was back on her feet, although she was still ordered by the new doctor to rest and not work. So Toy was filling in for her now that the clinic was opened again. He seemed smitten with Jacob.

And who wouldn't be? He was built like Dwayne Johnson and had muscles for miles. Jessi had never been into muscly men, but he still appreciated the sheer beauty of it.

Toy directed the two of them to one of the exam rooms. There was an old ultrasound machine in the corner. Apparently, the doctor brought it with him from Portland. Jessi helped Linc sit up on the exam bed and then leaned against the wall behind him. The room was bare besides a countertop and a rollie chair. They only waited a few minutes before the blond hair, blue-eyed doctor entered the room.

He smiled at them, "I'm Doctor Millerton, but please call me Jacob."

"I'm Jessi, and this is Linc," Jessi said, shaking the doctor's hand.

"Well, nice to meet you both," Jacob said. He shook Linc's hand after releasing Jessi's, and Jessi wanted to growl. *What the fuck! Possessive much?!* He chastised himself.

Linc was smiling, which was good. Jessi noticed that he wasn't shying away from alphas as much.

"So, how far along are you?" Jacob asked.

"About five months, I think," Linc responded.

"And you're not an alpha," the doctor stated to Jessi. It wasn't a question but a fact.

Jessi answered anyway, "no, what does that have to do with anything?"

"Well, in my studies so far, I've only ever seen omegas get pregnant from alphas."

"Oh, well, I'm not the biological father," Jessi said, correcting the doctor.

"But *he* wasn't an alpha either," Linc added. "He was an old-worlder."

"Hrmm. I'd like to do tests and take samples from the father then. I had—"

"That's not possible," Jessi said with a growl. "The bastard is dead." Linc squeezed Jessi's hand in support when Jessi tightened his hold on Linc's hand.

Lin turned to the doctor. "Sorry, Jessi's very protective of me. Harvey kidnapped me when I was a teenager and raped me for years. He was trying to impregnate me because his wife was sterile. I escaped two months ago after learning I was pregnant, and Jessi found me."

The doctor's face fell in horror, "oh my, I'm so sorry. I didn't know. I won't ask about him again."

"It's okay, doctor, you didn't know."

"Well, how about we see your baby," the doctor said, rolling over to the ultrasound machine. He flicked it on.

"I would love that."

The doctor took a few minutes to adjust the machine before he asked Linc to lie down. He placed a wand over his stomach that had cold goop on it. It sent a chill through Linc's spine.

"Sorry, I should have warned you."

Linc watched the screen in wonder as the doctor moved the wand around. Suddenly the room was filled with a *whoosh, whoosh*. "That's your baby's heartbeat," Jacob said with a smile.

Jessi was smiling brightly. It was beautiful. Linc wanted to reach over and pull him into a kiss, but he didn't have to because Jessi leaned over and kissed him sweetly. "That's our baby, sweetheart."

Linc's heart melted when Jessi called the baby *ours* instead of just his. He smiled against Jessi's lips before turning back to the doctor.

The doctor pointed out different blobs on the screen and took measurements. "Well, the good news is that the baby looks healthy and right around five months. Do you want to know the sex?"

"Yes!" Linc said right away.

The doctor pushed around on his tummy some more until he smiled. "It's a girl." He pointed to a section on the screen between the two legs. Linc and Jessi locked gazed and then kissed again before pulling apart. The doctor wiped away the gel from the ultrasound.

"There are a few things different about male versus female pregnancy."

The way he said it sounded concerning, "what is it doc? Linc's going to be okay right?"

The doctor rested his hand on his leg. "I'm going to do everything in my power to make sure every omega has a successful delivery. That being said, male omegas have a higher death rate and stillborn rate than women do. But I have a ninety percent success rate, which is the highest in the country."

"What causes these problems?"

"Most issues are towards the end; human males weren't designed to carry a child. But hopefully, the body will evolve as it has done in the past. Secondary sex traits, the alpha/omega genes, are just part of our most recent evolution. I predict that as time goes on, there will be fewer betas born. But that is yet to be determined. We will have to monitor this first generation of omega children. I'm uncertain yet, but my professional theory is they will either be alpha or omega."

"Wait, you can't tell if a child is going to be alpha, omega or beta now that you know there is such a thing?"

"Maybe in the future, we will, but when the babies are born, we only see their external physical traits. I have done ultrasounds on the babies after they are born, but I have yet to see different internal organs. I could do more invasive tests, but unless a baby has a problem, we don't want to do that. So, it's just safer to wait until their hit puberty to determine their secondary sexual trait."

"Okay, so what are their complications?" Jessi asked, directing them back to the topic at hand.

"Oh, sorry, yes. So, a male omegas body produces a plug that blocks the birth canal, the same as a female. The problem is that the birth canal on males connects to the colon. Any birth causes much stress on the body, and it stretches the colon. Any tears can cause major issues. In women, this is separate, so it's less of a complication. I recommend for that reason that we do c-sections whenever possible on male omegas."

"Okay, I'll do that then," Linc said. His face was pale, and he was a little shaky.

Jessi turned towards him, "Hey, look at me, the doc is just giving us information on what could happen. He's going to take real good care of you, okay?" Linc nodded, he was still pale, but he wasn't shaking anymore. "Did you want to go home, and I can get the rest of the information from the doctor?"

Linc squeezed Jessi's hand again, "no, I need to hear this."

It was Jessi's turn to nod. He pressed a kiss to Linc's lips before turning back to Jacob.

The doctor explained other complications of birth, including apparent preeclampsia. For some reason, male omegas had a higher chance of developing it than other symptoms.

Chapter 18

Iggy arranged for Jessi to work at the community kitchen instead of driving. Another alpha was taking over his truck route. Jessi was glad. He didn't want to be apart from his Linc, any more than he had to be, so working nearby and coming home would be lovely.

Linc would help him in the morning, but he could only work for a few hours before getting tired and had to go home. They had just finished cleaning up after lunch when he saw Linc waddle over to him.

"I'm going to go take a nap. I'll come back later?"

"You know you don't have to come back if you're too tired, right?" Jessi said, wrapping his arms around his boyfriend.

Linc pressed a kiss to Jessi's chin and leaned his head on Jessi's chest. "I know, but I enjoy cooking. It relaxes me."

Jessi lifted his chin and kissed his lips in a soft, closed-mouth kiss. He smacked his ass gently as he pulled away, "go on, get out of here. I'll bring dinner home."

Linc nodded and left. Jessi watched as he wandered off down the street, stopping to say hi to all his new friends. It had only been a few days, but Linc was really coming out of his shell.

"You're happy," Ada said, coming up beside him. The woman had curly black hair and gray eyes. They had known each other for years; she was his sous-chef back when he owned a restaurant. They had kept in touch once he started driving trucks. After Geoff's death, she moved here to be near him. "I don't even remember you being this happy with Geoff."

"I was happy, Ada. It's just different with Linc then it was with Geoff. It's a different type of happiness."

"Well, whatever it is, I'm happy to see it on your face."

"Thank you, what about you, how's your love life?" he asked. They had gone back to preparing the next meal. He was chopping onions while she was making the dough.

"Meh, no one's catching my interest. Maybe one day. John and I still get together occasionally, but that's about it."

Jessi shook his head. They continued discussing their lives as they worked. She gave him juicy details on what was happening with the community. Apparently, Toy had a crush for the new doctor, but poor Hana had been in love with that boy forever. So, who knew what was going on there?

Five hours later, Jessi walked into his small home. All the lights were off, so he sat dinner down and went to the bedroom. Maybe Linc had fallen asleep before it got dark when he switched on the bedroom light though the bedroom was precisely how it had been this morning, which meant that Linc hadn't taken a nap in the bed at all.

"Linc?" Jessi called out. He checked the kitchen for a note when he got no response, but there was nothing anywhere. *Okay, don't panic, Jessi*. He told himself. But he already felt the panic rising.

He pushed it back down, the dinner leftovers forgotten, he walked next door. He knocked on the door. "Jessi?"

"Mr. Matsudaira, have you seen Linc? He's not home, but he didn't leave a note."

The older man, Hana's father, shook his head, "no—wait, no, that's not true. I saw him heading this way, but then a woman stopped him. He turned around and went the other way with her. I haven't seen him since."

A bad feeling was sitting in Jessi's gut; what would a woman want with a pregnant omega, in any case? "Do you know who it was?"

"No, I don't know her name. She came to town a few months ago, though, I think. My Hana might know, hang on."

"Tell him to meet me at Iggy's."

Jessi didn't wait for a response. He left Mr. Matsudaira standing there and headed off to Iggy's. He needed to find his omega. His gut was telling him something was wrong.

On the way, he saw Tada walking towards him, "Hey, have you seen Linc?"

"No, man, I've been on duty all day on the west side. I'll let you know if I see him, though."

Jessi asked everyone he saw on the way to Iggy's. No one had seen his omega.

"Rei-chan," he said when the housekeeper opened the door.

"Jessi-san, what I pleasant surprise, where's that pretty omega of yours."

"I don't know, that's why I'm here. Is Iggy in?"

"Yes, Ichirou-san and Declan-san are in their room for the evening. I'll go get them; you know where the office is."

"Yes, ma'am." Rei let Jessi by, and he headed to Iggy's office. It didn't take long for the small alpha to join him with his sleepy omega by his side. Declan looked like he was asleep a few minutes ago; his hair was sticking in several ways.

"Jessi, what's wrong?" Iggy asked with a frown when he entered the room.

"Linc is missing. Hana's father said that he saw him disappear down the street with a woman when he was on his way back to the house to rest."

"And Matsudaira didn't know who she was?"

"No, he said that she showed up in town a few months ago."

"Okay, let's go." He turned to his fiancé, "go back to bed, baby. We'll find Linc."

He gave Declan a gentle kiss. The larger man huffed because he hated being treated delicately. "No, I'm only three months along, I can still help search."

Iggy sighed. Declan reminded Jessi of Geoff. "Fine," Iggy grumbled. The three of them, along with Benji, left the house, "get something that has his smell on it, like a dirty shirt. Benji should be able to trace it."

Jessi ran to his house. Hana and his father were standing outside, waiting for them. "Jessi, I'm so sorry, my father told me what happened. I had no idea."

"Hana, it's fine," Declan said, coming up behind them.

Jessi grabbed the pants that Linc had worn the night before and brought them back out.

"Well, good thing you trained Benji here as a tracker," Iggy said to Hana's father. "You've got another one training, right?"

"Yeah, but she's not ready yet. She'll run off on you as soon as she would track for you."

Iggy let Benji smell the shirt, Matsudaira-san, "where did you see Linc with the woman?"

The old man walked done about one-hundred yards and turned around, "they were right about here."

Iggy placed Benji on a leash. Which commonly he never did,

but Jessi guessed he needed to keep him close if they were going to track Linc. It made sense.

The dog sniffed around the spot, barked and then took off. He headed in the direction that Mr. Matsudaira remembers seeing them go. The dog followed the trail all over the place. Back and forth across the town. Jessi was giving up hope thinking the dog was mad when he finally left the city. A single woof before he started following a trail.

Chapter 19

Linc's face paled. Was he losing his mind? He had to be. He paused in the middle of the street, and she walked over, "come with me quietly, or I'll stab the baby," the evil woman said.

She dragged him around town. The paths she took ensured they'd stay away from guards and Jessi. Linc concluded that she had to have been in town for a while. And knew when guards were doing their shifts or something. The only people they saw where people that wouldn't realize that he was in distress.

He could feel the tip of the knife pushing into his stomach. So he believed her when she said one wrong move, and she'd kill the baby. After about an hour, she finally turned out of town, taking him into the forest.

She pushed him ahead of her "walk."

"What do you want, Shelley?" Linc asked the evil woman.

He was sure she was worse than Harvey ever was. No, she didn't rape him, but she let it happen all in the name of her getting a baby. She laughed when Harvey hit him repeatedly. Why didn't he ever think that she might come after him?

"What do you think I want? I wasted away in that God awful town for two months. You think I did it for your bratty ass?"

"You'll have to kill me before I let you have my baby, Harvey's dead. You have no one to beat me up for you anymore."

"Oh, you underestimate me, little Lincoln. Now shut your trap and walk."

Linc lost track of how long they walked, for he was exhausted. His feet hurt. He was about to pass out. When he tried to stop, Shelley would push him. He would fall forward, barely preventing himself from falling on his stomach.

He wrapped his arms protectively around his belly. Hopefully, someone saw them leave and would point Jessi in the right direction.

"In there," the evil bitch said with her nasally voice.

When Harvey first kidnapped him, Shelley pretended to be his friend. She acted like she was just as much of a victim as he was. So he opened up to her. It turned out she did that to get information for Harvey and use it against him. Her favorite thing to do was lock him in the bedroom for days at a time with nothing but water to drink.

She enjoyed watching her husband fuck Linc too. He always fucked him raw, no lube. She would sit in front of Linc and rub her stinky ass pussy in front of his face and often shoved his face in it.

He shivered at the thought of it. She tasted disgusting. He didn't see how Harvey could stand her smell, but again he didn't know how Harvey did half the things he liked to do.

They ducked inside a cave. She zip-tied his hands behind his back and his feet together so that he couldn't go anywhere.

As soon as the sun was up, they were moving again. The path was getting clearer like they were heading out of the woods. His lips were chapped, she'd only given him a few sips of water that morning, and that was all. He felt like he was going to pass out like he got no sleep at all.

They finally walked into a clearing, it was full of sunflowers, and there was a thin line of trees on the other side of it. Then past that, he could see a road. He also saw a car sitting next to the road. *Fuck!* How was Jessi supposed to find him if she took off in a car?

"Come on; we're almost there. Maybe if you behave, I'll let you live and take care of my little boy."

Girl! He said in his head. He smiled to himself, knowing that even if she got away with him, she wasn't ever going to get the boy she wanted. He'd get out just like he did the first time, *right?*

She shoved him through the tree line, and he fell to his knees. Just as he caught himself, he realized they weren't alone. Suddenly, he was being yanked back up by his hair. At least it was shorter now. He had it cut the other day, so he didn't have to worry about getting it in his face.

Shelley wrapped her arm around his neck and stabbed him with her blade. "Let us go, or he's dead."

"Let him go. You're surrounded," Jessi's voice called out.

"You might kill me, but are you going to take that chance with your pretty boy?" Shelley responded.

"I said—" Linc doubled over in pain, a cramp tore through him, and her knife tore through his throat. Linc heard several gunshots before he blacked out.

"Linc, sweetheart?" He could hear Jessi's voice through the pain fog, but he wasn't sure if he wanted to wake up the dark was comfortable. "Kitten, wake up for me."

Linc blinked up to see Jessi's face.

"Hey there, sweetheart, how are you feeling?"

"Hurts," he groaned. And the pain hurt. It felt like his stomach had been torn in two. "Baby?"

"Ssh," he realized that Jessi had tears in his eyes. "Fine, she's going to be fine."

Linc wasn't sure if Jessi was trying to convince Linc or himself. "Shelley?"

"Was that who that bitch was? She's dead. That was Harvey's wife, huh?"

"Yeah," Linc relaxed back into Jessi. He realized that they were in a car. His chest felt lighter. He hadn't even realized that he had been worried about Shelley coming after him. Yet, now that he thought about it, he felt stupid to believe that she never would.

"Where are we? How'd you find me?" Linc asked.

"What do you remember?"

He explained what happened from the time he left the community kitchen until they got to the street.

"Well, I knew there was something wrong the second I got home, but I figured you just feel asleep. When I couldn't find you, Iggy brought his dog in. She's trained as a tracker. So Iggy followed your trail through the night. When we realized where she was heading, half of us double-backed and searched the road. The stupid bitch didn't even try to hide her car. She must not have known that Benji was a trained tracker."

Linc inhaled sharply and reached from his stomach.

"What's the matter?"

"Hurts."

"We'll be back to Copperfalls in a minute. Jacob will check you and the baby out."

Linc reached for the pain in his neck.

"It was just a scrap, you're fine."

Linc relaxed his head on Jessi's should for a few minutes until the car stopped. Jessi carried him down the street to their home with Jacob on their heels. Toy and Declan were already in the bedroom with an IV bag ready for a saline drip.

"Hey, babe," Toy said with a sad smile. "Are you okay?"

Linc nodded. Toy's sass made him smile. He seemed so shy when Linc first met him, but once he got to know him the quirkier, he got turned on.

"Well, let's get you all fixed up." Toy went about setting up and IV for Linc. Linc decided that he did not like needles at that point.

"Jessi, can you go get the ultrasound machine from the clinic?" Jessi bent over and kissed Linc's forehead before leaving the room.

"Linc, I'd like to check your cervix. Can you pull down your pants?"

He nodded. Toy helped him pull the blanket over his knees, and he pulled his pants down. Jacob talked to him the whole time, telling him what he was doing. It felt weird. It wasn't intimate like Jessi's touches, just clinical.

A minute later, he pulled his hand out. "Well, you're not dilated at all, so that's good, but you lost your mucous plug, which isn't. You're going to have to stay on bed rest for the length of the pregnancy. Hopefully, these aren't contractions you're feeling. Let me know if you feel pain again."

Jessi returned a few minutes later with the ultrasound machine. Everything looked fine on the ultrasound, so they left Linc alone to rest and finish the IV.

Jessi doted on him the rest of the night. He made him dinner, read a book to him and rubbed his back until he passed out.

"I love you," Jessi whispered against his forehead as his dreams overtook him.

Chapter 20

After a few days rest, Linc was ready to get out of the house. He spent years stuck inside a tiny room. He wanted to be free. Unfortunately, now he was stuck on bed rest. Jacob had told him he could move about the house and cook meals, but that was about it. He wasn't allowed to have penetrative sex either. The doctor said hand jobs and blowjobs were okay and even beneficial for his health.

At least he only had four more months to go. He spent most of his adult life not knowing what he was missing. So five more months of not having Jessi's dick penetrate him should be doable. For Jessi's part, he doted on the omega whenever he was there. Toy stopped working for Kagiyama. With Yori incapacitated, Jacob needed help at the clinic. Toy jumped on the chance.

"Linc, babe?" Toy called out early one more about thirty minutes after Jessi had left for work.

"I'm in the bedroom," Linc called back. He was reading a book, so he sat it down when Toy walked in.

"Hey, princess." He learned that Toy had a flamboyant streak when he wasn't around the bulky alphas in town. Then he was almost as timid as Linc was.

Toy pulled his friend into a hug after setting bags on the ground. "I brought some stuff for baby Linc. I'm going to paint the baby's room," he said.

"Did you need help?"

Toy shook his head, "no, no preggers painting; it's a rule. The hot Dr. Jacob said so. So, you just sit here and look like your pretty little self. I'll be done before you know it." He kissed Linc's cheek. "Here, you can go through this and decide what you want to keep," he said, dumping the bag he brought on to the bed. "Declan's should be here shortly to keep you company while I paint."

Without another word, he stood up and left, his ass swishing back and forth as he went.

Linc shook his head and started digging through the items on the bed. There were all kinds of baby stuff, some of it he did not understand what it was he would have to ask.

About ten minutes into Linc's sorting, Declan knocked on the door before letting himself in. Even though he was two months behind Linc in gestation, they were about the same size. Linc was glad he wasn't the one having twins.

"Hey, man, how's papa?" Declan didn't hug Linc but sat down on the edge of the bed instead.

"Good, the baby's kicking, so she's happy. How are you?"

"Tired," he replied, and he looked it too. Linc couldn't imagine. He was only making one baby; two babies seemed surreal. "What's all this?"

"Toy brought it over. He said, pick what I wanted." Linc had set aside quite a few little girl onesies in all different sizes and some other things. Most of the stuff was clothes.

"What the heck is this?" Declan asked, he held up a bulb syringe and squeezed it.

"Not a clue," Linc responded. He made grabby hands as he wanted it, so Declan handed it over. He squeezed it a few times before setting it aside. "Nope, don't have a clue, Jessi probably knows."

"Toy," Declan called.

Linc raised his eyebrow at the other man.

Declan shrugged, "he might know since he was raised here."

Before Linc could respond, Toy peaked his head in the room; he had speckles of pink paint everywhere. "Well, I was going to ask you if you knew what this was," Declan started, holding up the bulb syringe. "But now I'm going to ask you if you even know how to paint. Jessi's carpet probably is covered in pink now."

Toy looked down at his shirt then back up at the other two boys, he shrugged. "I've got a paint tarp down, and these clothes are my painting clothes, see." He pointed out the speckles of darker colored paint that Linc and Declan hadn't seen before. "And that's a bulb syringe," he added, pointing at the discarded item in a pile.

"What the heck does it do?" Linc asked, picking it back up and squeezing it again.

"It sucks the snot out of a kid's nose."

Declan and Linc looked at each other and then wrinkled their noses.

Toy left and went back to painting. Declan helped Linc sort through the rest of the items, making two piles. Linc was going to keep the bulb syringe. He figured if people made something like that, it would be useful.

After they were done, they went to the living room and watched a movie. They spread out on the couches with many pillows and snacks. When they were done with the film, they made lunch and ate with Toy, who was finished with the painting.

Declan's mother came over with knitting needles and taught the boys how to knit in the afternoon. It was nice because it would give Linc something to do when Declan and Toy couldn't spend all day with him.

Finally, around five, Jessi came walking in the door with a rocking chair. "Hey, sweetheart." He said, leaning over Linc's comfortable spot on the couch and giving him an indecent kiss.

Toy smirked when he kissed Linc's cheek before leaving soon after. He dragged Mia and Declan with him, "leave the two of them alone," he chided to Mia.

Jessi sat down in Declan's vacated seat and pulled Linc into his lap. Their lips met in a sloppy kiss. Linc groaned and bucked against his lover; he had been horny all day. The doctor said the hormones would make him hornier than usual at this time in the pregnancy.

"Please," he whispered.

"Please, what?" Jessi replied.

"I don't know, I just need. I need you now. Please."

Jessi stood up, manhandling Linc with ease and made their way down to the bedroom. Linc had totally forgotten about the piles of baby stuff on the bed, but that didn't matter. Jessi pushed them on the floor.

When Linc protested, Jessi responded with, "I'll pick it up later."

Jessi undressed his omega and climbed between Linc's legs. He hovered over Linc and smiled down at him, "I love you, kitten."

Linc reached up and cupped his cheek, "I love you, too."

Jessi smiled brightly; it was the first time that Linc had said the words. He pressed a kiss to Linc's lips quickly before moved down the bed.

Jessi kissed the inside of Linc's thigh, making him wiggle. He repeated it on the other side before sucking one of Linc's balls in his mouth. His kitten sucked in a breath and moaned quietly.

His fingers ran along Linc's skin, dragging across Linc's baby bump. Gooseflesh rose as he went until he found Linc's nipple. With a twist and a pinch, Linc choked out a scream. "Please, Jessi."

Jessi smiled and kissed Linc's thigh again. He put Linc out of his misery and suck his cock into his mouth. Linc's cock was hard and pressed up against his baby bump, trying to point straight up. Jessi licked it several times before wrapping his mouth around the uncut head.

As he sucked on the tip, he ran his tongue underneath the foreskin. Linc shuttered and shouted out, "yes," as he continued to torture the boy shaft with his hands and mouth.

Jessi wet his fingers and pressed them against Linc's hole. He pushed as hard as he dared without pressing inside. His mouth swallowed Linc's cock and bobbed up and down.

"God, Jessi, oh, right—" Linc screamed. His back bowed off the bed as his balls tightened up. Jessi pressed Linc back down onto the bed and hallowed his cheeks. "Fuck!" Linc said as his orgasm washed over him. He pumped his hips twice, squirting his cum down Jessi's mouth.

When he was down, Jessi climbed up the bed and pulled his naked omega into his arms. Jessi held him until he fell asleep exhausted.

Thank You

Thank you for reading. As an Indie author, I rely on reviews and feedback. So please take a few minutes to leave a review.

I enjoyed writing about the giant lumberjack, Jessi and his skittish omega, Linc. When I first added Jessi to Iggy's story, he was literally just a voice on the phone. But then he needed a reason not to be able to find a doctor. Thus book two was born.

We've got babies coming in the next book. What will the new doctor, Jacob, do with two high-risk pregnancies? Can the help of one untrained omega and an old nurse be enough? Find out in Beta in Deep.

Japanese Terms

Hey All,

Here's a list of the Japanese terms I used throughout the book.

Segare—Son
Otōsan—Father
Okāsan—Mother
Oyabun—Boss
Wakagashira—Second in command
Shategashira—3rd in command
Wakagashira-hose—Enforcer leaders
Kumi-in - Enforcers
Otto—Husband
Kazoku—Family
Sakazuki—Ritual pledging loyalty

I used the Japanese characters below for the scene cuts.

Book 1 — オメガ — Omega

Book 2 — 逃走中 — On the run

Book 3 — ベータ — Beta

Lastly, these terms are added to the end of names for honorific purposes. The Japanese use these terms instead of terms of endearment. You may have noticed that Iggy uses a term of endearment for Declan; the alpha only reserves the honorific titles for the elderly (old-worlders).

-san added to the end of the name in a formal setting
-chan added to the end of a female's name in an informal setting
-kun added to the end of a male's name in an informal setting

Sneak Peek
Beta in Deep — Chapter 1

Toyama tossed his dildo across the room in frustration. *This is the last heat I'm spending alone,* he vowed. But he promised that every time he went into heat. His hand dildo wasn't just cutting it anymore. He needed the real thing.

As much as Toy silently pleaded for Hana to *see* him, the man seemed oblivious. He was the smartest person Toy knew, but that didn't stop the man from not seeing their connection. Toy had seen it since they were little boys, before they even knew they were different.

Hana was his, that's all there was to it. But Hana went out of his way to not cross that line. Toy should know he tried several times. Even when they were drunk, the man was stubborn. If Toy didn't know any better, he'd swear that man was an alpha.

Toy groaned as a hot flash spread up his chest. He'd just come not even five minutes ago. This was getting ridiculous. He looked down at his weeping dick, "give me a break, bitch."

He grabbed the remote and flipped the porn back on. They were allowed to use a certain amount of electricity in a day. When he was in heat, his mother found things to do outside the house and allowed him to use the television for porn, thank God. Not that it stopped Toy from thinking about his best friend.

His room was as any teenagers would be, lined with posters and random art he could find at the market. His bed was old and creaked when he climbed on it. He had a dresser and a single nightstand. Living in this room all his life, he had accumulated a look of random things, especially after he started scouting with Kagiyama.

Toy waited as long as he could before he lubed the worn dildo out and pushed it back inside of him. The men on the screen were pounding against each other. Toy imagined that he was the bottom, and Hana was behind him, and he moved up and down on his toy.

He let his cock bounce against his stomach as he got in a pleasant rhythm, fucking himself into a stupor. Because that was the only way he was going to get any sleep tonight.

He grabbed his dick when he was close to coming, jacking three times before spraying his seed across his bedspread. His cock stayed hard. He winced from the sensitivity, but he knew from experience that if he pushed through it, the pain would turn to pleasure again, and his balls would explode a second time.

So, he squirmed as he forced himself to speed up his strokes. Sweat dripped from his brow; the toy inside him was fully seated, but it wasn't enough. He reached behind him and added two fingers, scissoring his hole wider. "Fuck! Fuck!" he screamed as his dick shot off again.

Collapsing on the bed, he withdrew his fingers from his hole and then gently pulled the dildo out. He winced from the soreness three days of fucking did to him.

Would it be better with a partner? Would it be the same? Declan told him that the alpha knot was the most fantastic feeling in the world when he was in heat. But the love of Toy's life wasn't an alpha, so he didn't even want to think about how a knot would feel.

The only dick he ever wanted inside him was Hana's, so until Hana was ready, Toy would remain a virgin. He just hoped that Hana figured it out sooner rather than later.

Toy reached for Hana's pillow. Yes, he had stolen it from Hana's house, well not really stolen it but traded. He didn't think Hana ever noticed. But when Toy felt his heat coming, he would take one of his pillows while he knew Hana was working and switch it out for the one Hana slept on.

This helped Toy through his heat, believe it or not. "Hana," he sighed into the pillow.

As his eyes drooped closed to sleep, the sound of his satellite phone going off had him jumping from the bed. With both Hana and Iggy out-of-town trying to track down some doctor for Declan, Mura had given him a phone for emergencies. He never once expected it to ring, however.

"Hello?" he said into the phone.

"Toy," Hana replied, sounding relieved.

"What's wrong, babe?"

"You don't know?"

"Um, hello, no. Why would I be asking you if I knew?" he replied.

"Chill on the sass, Toy, I assumed that Mura would have filled you in right away," Hana responded, clearly annoyed. The man hated when Toy got sassy with him. Well, too bad, because that's who Toy was. He was full of sass. Secretly, Toy thought that Hana loved it.

"I'm kind of indisposed at the moment. I'm sure Mura would have filled me in tomorrow. But since you called, what's the emergency."

Toy grabbed his nail file off his nightstand and started cleaning his nails as he listened to Hana tell him what Mura had relayed to him. Toy would have gotten off the phone and gone to talk with Mura himself, but he rather talk with Hana. Besides, he had this stupid hangnail that was bugging him.

He sat the nail file down, though, when he heard another voice in the background. It was deep and husky. It was sexy as fuck, and he didn't recognize it. Instantly he was both jealous and turned on at the same time. He slapped his dick, willing it to go down.

"—so we'll be home in about ten—"

"Who the fuck is with you?" Toy asked, interrupting Hana.

If he could see Hana, he imagined the man was rolling his eyes. He hated when Toy interrupted him, but that only made Toy want to do it all the time. It was so fun to push his man's buttons.

"Toy," Hana whined, confirming Toy's suspensions that he was annoyed. "You know I hate that."

"I think," he said boldly. "That you really don't, you just pretend you do."

"No, Toyama, no, I really don't." Now Toy was annoyed. He hated when people used his full name, only his mama, Kagiyama, and the rest of the Japanese elders could get away with it.

He huffed, "Hanazawa, you know I hate when you use my full name. But you still didn't answer my question. Who the fuck is with you, babe?"

"Relax, it's just the new doctor. He's come home with us."

"He doesn't sound all that old."

"He's not. I think he's maybe in his thirties?" Hana replied.

Yuk. Toy knew Haha so well that just from his voice, he knew the man was lusting over the new doctor. "You want to fuck him, don't you?" Toy asked with annoyance. Hana got his dick wet with anyone willing except for Toy. It was the most irritating thing in the world.

"Toy, really? You're going there now? How many times have—"

"Nope, stop it, Hana," Toy said, cutting him off. Hana always had an excuse for why he had countless sex, but Toy didn't want to hear it, and Hana knew that much at least. "I don't want to hear it."

Toy kept his feelings for Hana close to his heart because he didn't want to get hurt. Was it better to be friends than nothing at all, right? At least that's what he kept telling himself.

"Sorry, Toy. I'll um; I'll see you when we get back, okay?"

Toy nodded as if Hana could see him before responding. "Okay." He hung up the phone with a heavy heart. Maybe he should just give Hana up. It had to be better than getting his hopes up every month, right?

Other books by Kaydee Robins

All books are available on Amazon in the Kindle Store and Paperback, except for the novellas.

The Eclipse Series

A Contemporary Military Romance
A Spy and his SEAL
A Cop and his Hacker
Two SEALs and their Hostage
A Marshal and his Witness
Box Set – Coming June 2021

Bonus Novellas
A Runaway and his Rock – Prequel
Only Available in the Box Set
An FBI Agent and his Partner – Book 2.5
Available on Prolific Works

The New Alphas Series

MPreg – A Contemporary Post-Apocalyptic Romance
Omega of the Enemy
Omega on the Run
Beta in Deep

Legends of the Packs

MPreg – A Contemporary Fairy Tale Shifter Romance
Ginger Fella
Caspian – Coming May 2021

About the Author

My name is Kaydee Robins. Reading has always been a passion of mine. In middle and high school, I would participate in the summer reading programs at the local library, often winning many prizes. My mom called me a hermit because I'd rather be in my room reading a book than outside or with my friends. I discovered my love for books in high school also extended to plays; thus, my passion for theatre was born. My favorite was working behind the scenes, creating colorful lighting effects.

I followed my passion in college and obtained an associate's in theatre arts. I also wrote short stories and fan fiction (don't judge). While I loved the theatre, I quickly learned that it wasn't practical to do for a living unless I got a break. So I started studying web and graphic design and did theatre as a hobby. Four years later, I had a bachelor's in information technology, followed by a master's a couple of years later. Today, I work as a system administrator in a NOC (network operations center), where I monitor my companies' network for server issues. Since a NOC is 24x7, I work in 12-hour shifts giving me literally half the month off to work on my hobbies.

In 2019, I decided that I was going to start writing again. My kids were finally old enough that I could concentrate more on my hobbies than theirs. I published my first book, *A Spy and his SEAL*, at the end of August. I design the covers for my books as well as edit them. Although one day, I hope I'll be able to afford a professional editor.

I learned long ago. I like reading all kinds of romances, straight, gay, bisexual; it doesn't matter. My favorite being gay paranormal. Nothing beats a good book about fated mates, shifters, and male pregnancy. Another top pick of mine is action/suspense romance. What's better than falling in love while dodging bullets and saving lives?

As for my personal life, I am a cisgender straight woman. I am married to a wonderful man who supports me for my weird habits and interests. He is a stay at home dad taking care of our daughter and two sons. When I'm not working, I'm reading, writing, playing video games, or watching my favorite dramas. I also bake bread, mainly sourdough, and have started using my starter in just about any baked products.

Follow Me

Facebook - https://facebook.com/kaydeerobins
Instagram - https://www.instagram.com/kaydeerobins
Twitter - https://twitter.com/KaydeeRobins
Good Reads - https://amz.run/3oE8

Contact Me

Email - kaydeerobins@outlook.com

Visit my Website

https://kaydeerobins.wordpress.com

Printed in Great Britain
by Amazon